MW00423129

ISLAND OF BONES

A
HAUNTED FLORIDA
NOVEL

GABY TRIANA

Copyright © 2018 Gaby Triana

All rights reserved. No part of this book may be reproduced in any form or by any electronic or mechanical means, including information storage and retrieval systems, without permission in writing from the publisher, except by reviewer, who may quote brief passages in a review.

ISBN: 9781983063329 (Paperback Edition)
ASIN: B07D7RQ4K2 (eBook Edition)
Characters and events in this book are fictitious. Any similarity to real persons, living or dead, is coincidental and not intended by author.

Book cover and interior design by Curtis Sponsler

Printed and bound in the United States of America
First printing April 2018

Published by Alienhead Press
www.alienheadpress.com
Miami, FL 33186

Visit Gaby Triana at www.gabytriana.com

ONE

1951

A weathered old officer from the Key West Police Department stood on my front porch, cigarette clenched between his teeth. "Leanne Drudge?"

"Yes?" I pushed the screen door open, wondering what this was about.

"I'm Officer Brady. This here's Officer Smith." He gestured to a younger man in uniform standing by the patrol car on the street.

"What can I do for you gentlemen?" The shrimp in garlic sauce would burn on the stove if he didn't make this quick.

"Your husband's been in a fatal boating accident." He checked the papers in his hand. "Treasure hunting off the coast of Cuba. On behalf of Monroe County PD, we're very sorry for your loss. We'll need you to come down to the station tomorrow. After you've had a moment to process, of course."

My chest heaved, and my mind erupted into a thousand questions, but I refused to believe him. I gripped the screen door with both hands to keep from falling. "I...I don't understand."

"Your husband's dead, Mrs. Drudge." He spoke with the sensitivity of saw grass.

Yes, I got that part. I just couldn't understand *how*.

Fatal boating accident? Bill was the best boat captain

1

in town. He navigated the seas like he did his wife— carefully. I wasn't the easiest person to deal with, but he listened for the right breezes, searched good and proper for storm fronts, knew when to avoid thick clouds, when to spearhead right through them. He wouldn't have had a boating accident any more than he'd have accidentally forgotten to make my heart and body long for him every day and night he was away.

As the officers waited, an early morning conversation from two days ago haunted me. "Today's the day, Leanne, baby. I can feel it!" Bill had said, excited about his boating trip. He'd been studying the precise location of a lost Spanish galleon, Nuestra Señora del Pilar, for the last seven years. It was his chance to become more than just a lobster fisherman.

But something wasn't right. I felt it in my soul—a darkness.

I hadn't known how to tell him. He wouldn't have listened anyway. "Now, Leanne…" he would've said, "this isn't the time for your mumbo jumbo."

My intuition. It'd always been right in the past, and I should've stopped him from going. Now I looked at Officer Brady without words, and it all made sense.

"I can see you're in shock, Mrs. Drudge. I'll send someone else over, one of the ladies from the station, or—"

"I'm fine." My hand shook on the screen door. My world would never be the same again. What about our dreams? What about Mariel asleep in her crib? What was I supposed to do now?

Officer Brady glanced at the other patrolman by the car who smiled and nodded at him, a silent idea communicating between them. He turned back to me. "In that case, uh…" He removed his cap, pressed it against his chest. Rise of his left eyebrow. Taunting. Pushing limits. "Mind if we come in?"

I gaped at his lecherous brown eyes roving over me. Would the people of this town stop at nothing to judge me? Suddenly, I feared his authority with Bill nowhere near to save me. "No. Thank you for coming." Quickly, I closed the screen and locked the door.

For a long time, I stood there, staring at the door, feeling my world collapse around me. Then, I willed my feet to move and wandered through the house in a fog. I reached my bedroom and the bed's edge, sat staring at my reflection while the baby slept. He couldn't have perished. Not in a boating accident.

No, no. This was wrong, this was impossible.

I stood and moved to the kitchen to pour a shot of whiskey, then took it outside into my garden by the inlet. Downing the shot, I stared at the water. It took a moment, but the wave rising behind my chest finally spilled over. It rose until the tears formed, until I looked at the moon sculpture Bill had carved for me, thought I would die if I didn't let out the pain.

With a wail, I cursed at God. Told him it was no wonder I never believed in him in the first place. What kind of merciful god would do such a thing to a young woman with a baby? A good god would make sure my husband came home. And if he couldn't find that treasure he'd been searching for all his life, then he'd at least trap a few lobster to help pay the bills.

There was no God, just like there was no truth.

And now, there was nothing worth living for either.

Only my baby.

In the coming weeks, Bill's death was a well-publicized "fact" in Key West, even though there wasn't a scrap of evidence. But women like me, we don't take things at face value. We look past the smirks of the fact-people—the reporters, the police. We search beyond the veil. I'd even say we "know" things other people can't explain.

It wasn't no boating accident.

We never saw him again, Mariel and me, and the months dragged by with achingly slow precision. My one-year-old quickly forgot the spark of her father's laugh. She stopped glancing at the door in the evenings. And because my life had been cursed the day Bill disappeared at sea, I even lost my family home.

As a widowed mother with no income of her own, I was forced to sell the only tangible thing I had—*Casa de los Cayos*—the twenty-eight-year-old house where I'd grown up, married my husband, made Mariel out of love. I lost it to Susannah McCardle, of all people.

My neighbor, Susannah, had wanted my house from the moment her daughter, Violet, got married last year. A dozen times she'd asked me when I'd planned to move. She wanted to expand, move her daughter in next door, she told me. Make a family compound of the two homes.

Never was always my reply. This was *my* house, and my mama's before me.

Susannah would scoff and head indoors but always come back out for a smoke. My house needed paint, she'd argue. It needed TLC, a man to care for it whereas that lazy SOB of mine had done nothing but boat and chase gold, and now look at where that had left me. I should just sell it and move to a cheaper key, she'd tried convincing me.

I held on as long as I could—another year. Finally, I couldn't make payments no more. Only so many jars of key lime marmalade sold before the bank account ran dry.

Susannah had won in the end. Now, her son-in-law who cut coquina for a living and her hateful bitch daughter, who did nothing but sit on her ass, would live in *my* house.

The shame hurt so bad, it burned a hole in my chest.

With Mariel in my arms, I crossed the gravel front yard, transporting the last of my belongings, stuffing as much as I could into the old Ford. The little girl from down the street watched me from her cross-legged position on the curb.

From her porch, Susannah watched with that over-plucked high eyebrow of hers. "Told you he would bite the dust out there, leave you like this." She sucked on her cigarette. "Probably ran into pirates or something."

"Shut up, Susannah. Nobody asked you."

"It's better this way, darlin'." She blew smoke into the late summer air and picked tobacco fragments from her teeth.

Meanwhile I tried to make the bicycle I'd bought a few years ago with the money I'd earned waitressing fit in the back. It wouldn't. "You want this?" I asked the little girl witnessing my shame. She stood and gaped, hardly believing I was offering up such a good thing. The bright blue bike was too big for her, but hell, she'd grow into it. Nodding, she took it off my hands.

The mosaic table Bill made me wouldn't fit into the truck either. Even Mariel tried telling me this with her big green eyes. *Mama? Let it go.*

How could I? He'd meticulously placed each piece of glass with his loving hands. I rested my head on the truck door, wanting to sob pathetically, but I quickly collected myself. I would not let Susannah have the glory of seeing me this way. I'd make this table fit in the car if it killed me.

"It's not going to fit, Leanne. Just leave the damn table behind."

"I'll decide what doesn't fit!" I spit. If I could've cast a swarm of flying daggers at her face, I'd have done it.

Damn it, the table wouldn't fit.

From her front porch, Susannah snickered.

Maybe after I got my life together in Plantation Key, I could save money, return to Key West, and buy back my house. "Don't get too comfortable," I told her, reluctantly leaving the mosaic table on the sidewalk. "I'll be back for it soon."

"Over my dead body, you will..."

Panting in the August heat, I paused to look at her. I absorbed her ugliness and toxic energy. The image would never be erased from my memory as long as I lived. Queen Victorious was most pleased now that this simple woman was not only heartbroken, but emotionally decimated as well. Why did she and everybody else hate me so? Because I didn't go to church? Because I felt more spiritual sitting in my herb garden than this town would ever be kneeling in the pews?

Over my dead body...

Yes. Maybe it would take that. But her dead body wasn't up to me. My mother had taught me that we didn't cause harm on others. Karma would take care of that. But I was also tired of living by the rules and getting screwed in the end. Tired of watching others' ships come in when mine was still lost at sea.

I closed my eyes and visualized Susannah McCardle's dead body, rotting, festering in the summer heat. Flies flitting into her mouth laying eggs. The police department knocking on *her* door. My house on the market again. Me earning it back. I could bend my mind around these visions, but I'd never been very good at manifesting dreams, or else my husband would still be here. I could only hope that Mariel would learn my mother and grandmother's ways better than I ever could.

Susannah tapped the porch railing. "Hello, Earth to Leanne." Her crooked smile matched her flyaway, graying hair.

Violet stepped onto the porch in curlers and short shorts, tapping her pack of cigarettes. "What's going on?"

"Leanne's finally leaving."

"About time."

I wouldn't give them the satisfaction of a reply. I plopped into the grass to pet our black kitty. "We can't take you with us, Luna," I whispered. "Apartments don't allow magical creatures." I smiled on the verge of tears. Mariel reached out to Luna, too.

I closed my eyes to visualize.

I imagined no happiness—zero, not a single scrap of it—ever entering *Casa de los Cayos* again as long as I wasn't there to make it happen it. Mariel clung to me, so still, eyes wide. Baby girl knew what I was up to, already learning, showing respect for the craft. Wondering what sorcery Mama was conjuring up this time.

"May this house and all who live in it suffer." My voice shook. "For without us, it is no longer a home."

Blowing out slowly, I envisioned my charged breath traveling, crossing the lawn and curling around Susannah, Violet, and the entire McCardle Family. It snaked over to my property and enveloped that too. As I belted in Mariel and stepped into the driver's seat, cranking on the engine, I stared at Susannah one last time. It was hard to ignore the victory in her eyes.

My lovely pink and white home, like the inside of a conch shell, seemed to sag just then. It called to me, begged me not to go. Not to worry, I would make things right, even if it took a lifetime. I would be back, whatever it took.

"So mote it be," I whispered then drove off down Overseas Highway.

TWO

Present Day

Miles away, Nana fell into a coma, as my boyfriend got down on one knee.

Not to propose riverside at the Museum of Science in Boston, no. That would've been cute and romantic, considering it was where Zachary and I had first met two years ago this very night. It was to pick up my IMAX ticket that had fallen out of my pocket, and the look on his face said it all.

"Ellie, we need to talk."

Ugh, famous last words.

I'd worried about this happening so much over the last month, sometimes I felt I'd caused it. Now here we were, staring at the St. Charles River, and I could almost envision everything he was about to say like a script in a bad, made-for-TV movie.

"This has nothing to do with you," he assured me. "It's me. I think…I think I need to be alone for a while." He wasn't sure what he needed, what he wanted, he added. Some time off would help him figure it all out.

I sat there avoiding the deep hazel eyes I'd never get lost in again.

For two years, I'd given my energy to Zachary when I could've spent that precious time with my ailing grandmother. Two years wasted. When he was done with his monologue, he asked if we could stay friends, and I gave him the middle finger.

That night at my grandmother's bedside, I deleted him off all social media, because who needed Zachary Dum-Dum Bowman condescendingly telling me I'd always be in his heart? Meanwhile he commented on Amada Payne's posts at least eighteen times a day. Didn't know what he needed, my ass.

I took Nana's wrinkled, lukewarm hand and pressed my cheek to it. "You were right. You're always right, Nana." She didn't move or acknowledge me.

Nana always said I'd know when the right man came along. I'd know because he'd adore me the way my grandfather adored her. He'd kiss me passionately before leaving home. There'd be a sparkle to his eye. I was lucky if I could get Zachary to put down his phone during dinner, much less look at me in any special way.

"But no offense, Nana...that kind of love doesn't exist anymore."

I should've been here when she slipped away. I should've listened to her mutter stories about the old days, about that house in Key West, about a mural designed in ocean colors, and an island I'd only seen in one faded photo. A house that'd haunted her dreams until a few days ago when she'd whispered its name in her sleep—*Casa de los Cayos*.

Instead, no thanks to Zachary's sorry ass, I hadn't been at her bedside to say goodbye. I never saw those green eyes again. Nana died in her sleep two weeks later.

When my mother told me that my grandmother had left me a small sum of money, enough to keep me alive a couple of months, I quit my job at the middle school two weeks before classes began. My principal wanted to know where she was going to find a remedial math teacher at this late hour, but I just couldn't deal.

I needed to get over losing Nana, Zachary, my worthless life. To get over how stupid and blind I'd been for two years. I needed a reboot on life, and I was pretty sure how I wanted to start.

Sitting at my mother's kitchen table, I stared at the brown box containing Nana's cremated remains. Inside the box wasn't just my grandmother, but every story she'd ever told me, every memory she'd ever recalled.

"What do we do with all her stuff in storage?" I asked.

Mom unfolded her hands, waved them around. "Keep whatever we want. The rest we sell or give away. She didn't have much, Ellie." She refolded her hands.

"I know." Nana had worked most of her life. First as a receptionist, then as a lunch lady at my mom's middle school in Key Largo, then they moved to Fort Lauderdale, then Savannah, then honestly, I had no idea how they ended up in Boston.

But it was clear she was never the same after my grandfather died, because my mother always talked about growing up with a sad woman who'd always longed for her childhood home. For an idyllic life she'd had with my boat captain grandfather before he disappeared. When I was little, I used to dream about this old life of hers— literally dream of colored tiles and glossy palm fronds, of drinking lemonade on a wooden porch, of a black cat whose name I never knew. I always woke up feeling like I'd actually been there.

"All she ever wanted was to return to Key West." My mother scoffed. "For all the good the island did her."

I stared at the brown box. "Then, let's take her back."

"I don't want to," Mom said, point blank. "She had so many bad memories there, I just can't."

"But it's where you were born. It couldn't have been all bad," I argued.

"One thing has nothing to do with another, Ellie," Mom said.

For years, I'd been trying to get us to visit Nana's old house in Key West. After all, she'd spent so much time reminiscing about it, I was pretty sure she would've wanted to see it one last time before she got worse.

"I feel like the place is cursed, Ellie. I can't explain it," Mom added.

Ugh. I was twenty-six years old and still hearing my mother talk about gut feelings she couldn't explain like they were any kind of evidence.

Mom shook her head. Her frustration was palpable. "Maybe we can send her ashes and hire someone to scatter them for us. I mean, I don't even know where the hell *Casa de los Cayos* even is, and—"

"I'll do it," I said.

"What?"

"I'll go. I'll figure it out. I have nothing else to do."

"But school starts in a few days."

"Mom, I quit."

"You what?" Bright green eyes stared at me like I'd lost my mind. And maybe I had. But I had a bachelor's degree in advanced mathematics, for goodness sake, I could find a job anywhere when I got back.

"Mom," I sighed. "Let me go to Key West. Nana would flip out if she knew you hired some random nobody to scatter her ashes. I'll find the house, I'll scatter them…maybe I'll even connect with Nana somehow."

Connect was a word my mother would understand. She'd been more spiritual when I was growing up, though nowadays, she seemed to be too busy for meditation and incense. She visibly relaxed. "Are you sure?"

"Yes. Positive." I smiled. "It'll be good for me. Help me forget ass-face."

"Oh, Ellie. Don't call him that."

"Mom. Just—don't."

For the first time in a while, I had something exciting to look forward to. A trip to Florida! I hadn't learned enough about Nana in the time I'd had her here. I hadn't asked the right questions, hadn't heard all the tales. I'd been too busy.

Besides, in the last two weeks, my covert OCD had kicked into high gear, giving me night terrors I hadn't had in a long time. This little getaway would be just as much for me as it'd be for Nana. I was on a plane to Miami the very next day, new bikini in my carry-on, Nana's ashes in my bag. Soon, I'd be sipping lemonade in a rocking chair watching the sun go down over paradise.

Tropical vacay, here I come.

THREE

Deep wrinkles covered his leathery face, and though there was nothing particularly scary about him, I wanted to run in the opposite direction. Who was he? The man followed me, crept closer, like he wanted to speak to me, except he wouldn't utter a word.

I felt the familiar sleep paralysis in my chest. I screamed but my cries blended with a pitchy, metallic whine somewhere in the distance. The distance? No, nearby. I jolted upright, swinging at the man's face to get away.

My eyes opened. I was sitting in an airplane, my face wedged between the seat and the fiberglass window. I was on the airplane to Miami, listening to the engines making their descent. The vibration of landing gear signaled that we were almost there. I panted, looking around. I'd startled the older lady next to me. "You okay?" she asked.

"Yeah." I pressed a hand to my chest. "I get nightmares. Sorry."

"My husband does too. Anxiety?"

"Not exactly."

It was hard to explain. I didn't feel like getting into it. Since I was a child, I'd had visions, sometimes awake, sometimes sleeping. Faces, people around me, shadows lurking just outside my peripheral vision. Sometimes I'd hear them speak. In my early teens, doctors told my mom these were classic signs of OCD. Not the same OCD that made people line things up in perfect rows, but *covert* OCD.

This was more internal. I had to line up my thoughts just right to get rid of the chaos, the negativity, the crippling self-doubt. I looked for order, smiles, and pleasant situations to counter the darkness. Probably the reason math and science had always felt good to me. Solid things I could count on. No "mumbo jumbo," as my grandmother called gut feelings. I'd been taking Zoloft for sixteen years now to help. Ever since...no visions, no negative thoughts, just a pleasant evenness.

On some days—numbness.

But ever since Nana died, this one vision had crept his way back into my dreams. He was Native American and harmless, but a moment ago, I'd sworn he was after me. Stupid brain.

"Flight attendants, prepare for landing," a female voice announced.

I pulled my purse from under the seat and plucked out my pill bottle. Only three sertraline left. I'd have to order more when I got to Key West. Breaking one with my fingernail, I figured I could use an extra half right now.

"Headed home or visiting?" My chatty seatmate wanted to know.

I cracked open one eye. "Visiting Key West."

"Oh, how nice! You'll absolutely love it. *Cayo Hueso*," she said.

Opening both eyes this time, I swiveled to face her. "Pardon me?"

"Key West in Spanish." She smiled. "Island of Bones, its original name."

"Oh. I didn't know that." I held my bag close, the

15

one containing my nana's remains—ashes and shards of bone in a box. How appropriate. The plane touched down. "Almost there, Nana," I muttered.

"Changes in latitudes, changes in attitudes, nothing remains quite the same," I sang behind the steering wheel of my rental Prius. Would I have preferred a convertible Mustang like half the cars taking the three-hour trip from Miami to Key West on this gorgeous summer day? Yes, but I also needed to make sure my grandmother's money lasted me at least two months, so I didn't have to hurry back to Boston right away.

As the Jimmy Buffett song suggested, my state of mind completely changed once I hit Overseas Highway, the single lane (sometimes double) road cutting through the Florida Keys. The brilliant sun, bright blue sea, and bite of salt in the air was enough to almost wash away the memories of the last month, like a good, strong gargle dislodging a heavy yuck in my throat.

Mangroves, beaches, and fishing piers rolled by. I tried to imagine Nana and Mom living here when they were younger. Mom had been born in Key West, but they'd relocated to Plantation Key after my grandfather died. Mom said she was too young to remember him, but Nana reminded her often of how much he loved her, played with her, and sang to her in the evenings.

For me, this was another world—a living postcard with brightly painted wooden houses on stilts, giant conch shells notifying passersby of tourist traps, and parrot-shaped windsocks blowing in the breeze. It was hard to imagine this corner of the universe as anything cursed, like my mother had suggested, but then again, the grass was always greener on the other side.

When it came time to drive across the seven-mile

bridge, part of me almost pulled over. My fingers gripped the steering wheel. Driving across the Florida Straits with nothing on either side but miles and miles of open ocean—*fan-freakin-tastic*. Behind me, an impatient driver rode my ass. I glared at him in the rearview mirror.

"You can do this, Ellie. Everyone else is."

Picking up speed, I told myself this was just another jaunt on the 495 back home, heading to Martha's Vineyard for the weekend. It was hard to believe that people used to take a train out here in the 1800s, that they even lived this far from the mainland. Hard to believe that anyone in settler times rode their horses and pulled their carts as far as Key West. How had they hopped across the islands without these bridges?

Boats. They traversed in boats, Ellie—duh.

Once I realized I wasn't going to plummet to my watery death, it was easy-peasy the rest of the way. *See? No doomsday.*

Thirty minutes hopping over more tiny isles, and I drove across one last short bridge making it to a traffic light. The colorful sign in the median read, *Welcome to Key West, Paradise USA.*

"I made it," I muttered, checking the time. "Holy shit, I made it."

If I hurried, I could also make it in time to watch the famous Key West sunset while holding a fruity adult beverage in hand. But I hadn't researched the best place to do that, hadn't made any hotel reservations either. I'd figured I could just pop into a Holiday Inn or Motel 6 when I arrived.

Mistake.

Every chain hotel I stopped at either didn't have vacancy or did, but at anywhere from $400-700/night for a basic room, I wouldn't be on vacation for long. I should've come with a plan. I should've thought this through.

I should've, should've, should've.

I stopped chastising myself long enough to find my way downtown to a place called Mallory Square. There I could grab a drink, watch the sun go down, and think about my Plan B. Parking wasn't easy, but the nice thing about a Prius was you could cram it anywhere, so I did between two doorless electric buggies. Getting out, I locked up the car and headed toward sounds of drunk people partying. A fluffy chicken hopped out of nowhere and clucked at me. A big rooster followed her, giving me the evil eye.

"Oh. Hey, chickens," I said, because chickens roaming freely was so normal, right?

Another world, indeed.

At Mallory Square, I bought myself a rumrunner from a street vending cart then parked my butt on a bench to watch the sun descend behind a small island out in the water. Dark silhouettes of sailboats cut out triangular shapes in the tangerine sky, and I let out the biggest sigh ever.

"I made it to the end of the world." That was how it felt, coming out this far south. Lifting my drink to the sunset, I said, "Welcome home, Nana."

Did she and my grandfather ever sail at sunset? Did my mother ever ride on a boat with them? After all, my grandfather had supposedly been a skilled boat captain, though I believe that was also how he'd died. So many things I'd never know. So many things I'd failed to learn about my family, my heart ached.

I soaked in the lazy vibes and party atmosphere, the ocean waves swishing just a few feet from me. Paradise USA was right. *Well worth the drive, Ellie?* I heard my grandmother ask from a distant place.

Well worth the drive. I smiled.

Once the sun sank and the tourists cheered, the nighttime party began. People, vendors, performers on stilts juggling bowling pins all filled the streets making me smile but also feel sad for some reason. Nana had grown up here in the what…1930s, 40s? I did some quick math in my head. She had to have left town in 1952 when my mother was only a year old. Had the island been as touristy back then, or had she lived here during some idyllic era of peace that no longer existed?

Nostalgia for a place I'd never know hit me hard.

The drink wasn't helping either. Everyone had someone to party with, and I was alone with a ghost in my purse and memories of a place I'd never been. How would I find *Casa de los Cayos* on this eight-mile-wide island? I didn't have to find it tonight, I reasoned. Tonight, I only needed to find a place to sleep then start my search tomorrow.

I stopped at a kiosk that sold gelato on one side and vacation timeshares on the other. "Excuse me." I stopped in front of a middle-aged woman with platinum blond hair up in a tight ponytail wearing bright pink lipstick. "Do you know any hotels with vacancies, not too expensive?" I asked. Maybe the locals could point me in a better direction than all-booked Expedia could.

"Did you try up on US-1?"

"Is that the road I drove in on?"

"Yes, the only road in. There should be some places out there. The farther away from center of town, the cheaper."

"Right, there weren't any. But thanks," I said, my hopes slumping. I'd already stopped at those places and they'd wanted an arm, leg, and my spleen for a night's stay.

"Miss?" The woman called me back. The man minding the gelato stand had apparently heard us talking. "La Concha Inn on South Roosevelt. That's the road on the left side of the island when you come in. You probably followed traffic to the right."

"I did. Thank you."

"They might have rooms during summer," she added with a cautious smile. She and the other attendant exchanged glances.

"Great. Thanks again." Walking in the direction of my car, I spoke into my phone. "Find La Concha Inn," I said, while British Siri searched for results. She showed me a location way on the east side of the island about as far from the good stuff a place could get.

Twenty minutes later, I'd arrived at the blue pinpoint on my map. At first, I wasn't sure this was the right spot, as it seemed to be a private home behind a gate surrounded by wild, unkempt foliage. Two stories, wooden columns with porches on both levels, ceiling fans that hung crookedly, the main house had seen better days. On either side were smaller homes like bungalows or cabins sitting in darkness—a compound of buildings. The front lawn had once boasted 70s-style kitschy Florida eye candy to attract tourists—a faded, peeling statue of a conch shell, an equally dilapidated parrot, and a pirate with not only his leg and eye missing, but his power to amuse as well.

I felt sorry for the statues like I felt sorry for the home. It didn't make sense to feel sorry for a structure, but the house looked like an old woman all alone at Bingo Night.

Turning off the car lights, I stepped out, my sandal crunching onto gravel. No big signs, no neon lights, no commercial draw-in of any kind, but the map insisted that this was La Concha Inn and didn't "la concha" mean shell in Spanish? I glanced at the shell statue again. *Yep.*

I grabbed my purse, leaving my suitcase in the car. Pulling back the chain link gate, I walked underneath a thick cover of trees, vines, and coconut palms in various states of growth. A small wrought-iron bench sat rotting underneath the moonlight, and sun-dried plastic toy cars littered the overgrowth. Ahead of me, something reptilian scuttled across the path. *Hello, Florida.*

The main home was poorly lit and needed a few coats of paint and serious refurbishing. It almost seemed to be leaning to one side. I couldn't tell what color it currently was because of the darkness, but it definitely didn't look bright or cheery like other places in town. It also didn't look open for business.

I was ready to call the listed number when the front porch light turned on. My heart pounded when I heard the screen door slowly creak open. A gaunt, braless woman appeared from the darkness wearing shorts and tank top, sallow skin like worn cowhide, cheeks sunken like spoons, and long hair like gray straw. "We're open," she croaked in a voice coated with nicotine.

Clearly, she was talking to me, though not attempting any eye contact whatsoever. "Awesome," I said, unsure that I wanted to proceed. I'd seen horror films that began this way.

If I decided I didn't like the way the establishment looked on the inside, I could always thank her and be on my merry way. There was nothing to this, yet I felt apprehensive heading up the steps. The stress of the last month had clearly spurred old anxieties. It didn't help that I'd traveled all day and been up since five this morning either.

I stepped through the screen door, greeted by a large gray cat with golden eyes who stood perfectly still like a live sculpture. Dusty fake bromeliads filled the small foyer and the smell of cigarettes permeated the air. I refused to believe that a hotel could be this bad and wondered if it was really just someone's ill-kempt house, but judging from the brochures haphazardly arranged in a plastic display case, it was a real place of business.

"You looking for a room?" the woman asked, coming to stand behind a counter to my left. She still wouldn't look at me, which was both rude and unnerving.

"Yes, but I wasn't sure if you were open for business. You should have a sign out front or something."

"Broke during Hurricane Irma. Haven't put a new one up yet."

"Oh, sorry to hear that. So, how much for a night?"

"Two hundred," she replied, "but I can give you a special rate if you stay three or more nights. Hundred-twenty a night." Her fingers drummed the countertop. No smile. No enthusiasm. Behind her, a much older, dark-skinned woman slowly plucked a paper cone from the side of a water dispenser and glanced at me. No smile from her either but then again, she looked like a woman who'd lived a long, hard life.

I wasn't sure I wanted to stay three nights. Maybe tomorrow I could try my luck closer to town and find a more appealing stay. This place looked like it'd seen better days and it wasn't like the innkeeper was doing backflips to be accommodating either.

"Breakfast is included," she added, as if that would seal the deal. The eye contact came then, as though she'd realized she'd have to work a little harder to get my money. There was something off about her dark eyes.

"At what time?" I asked.

"Six-thirty to nine-thirty." Her left eye didn't move. Was positioned differently. It might've been a glass eye, giving her the appearance of a broken animatronic.

I wouldn't be awake until ten-thirty, but I had nowhere else to go, so I bit the bullet. "Let's go with one night to start. If I like it, I'll be happy to pay two more at full price." Even at $200 a night, it was cheaper than everywhere else and staying here would keep me from booking on another island and having to drive here daily.

The woman nodded and clacked at her old keyboard while I picked a few brochures. The Hemingway House, the Southernmost Point, Sunset Spooks Ghost Tours... The big gray cat jumped up onto the counter, scaring the shit out of me.

"Geez," I caught my breath.

"He likes you," the woman grunted. "He doesn't like anybody."

"Well, hello little guy. You scared me." I petted the cat's head. At first, he wasn't sure if he wanted my human hands all over his dusty pelt, but then he leaned into my palm and purred rhythmically. The sound was the only comforting thing about this place.

"It's Bacon."

"Excuse me?"

"The cat's name," she said. "Bacon."

"Bacon?" I coughed a nervous laugh and pet the kitty who rubbed his cheek so hard against my hand, he left a trail of saliva across my thumb. Ew. "Does he show up to breakfast or wisely stay away?" I snorted. "You know...Bacon?"

She stared at the ancient computer screen.

I swallowed and dropped the jokiness. "I've never been much of a cat person," I said. Mrs. Friendly didn't look like she cared one bit about anything I had to say.

Just hand over my two hundred dollars. I didn't know why I was being so chatty. I just felt like at least one of us should be filling the silence.

After a minute of taking my information, she pulled a key on plastic ring from a drawer and handed it to me. I'd never stayed anywhere that didn't use a key card. "You'll be staying in Room 2. It's through those doors, follow the garden path to your right, then the second door to your right. Double bed, bathroom, access to the garden, and TV."

"Is there a Wi-Fi password?" I asked.

"You'll get a decent signal with your regular phone service."

So, that was a *no.* "Okay, then." I took the key and tapped the counter. "Thank you so much. What was your name again?" In case I wanted to write a terrible review on Trip Advisor later.

"Syndia Duarte."

"Ms. Duarte, thank you," I said, noting the dour looks from both her and the old woman sitting like a wax figure in the chair behind her. Shaking them off, I turned to go. I was halfway through the living room with Bacon at my heels when it occurred to me that both these women were locals. Either might've heard of the home I'd come here searching for. I turned back around just as she was shutting off the light to her office. "Oh, Ms. Duarte? Would you happen to know where I might find a residence on the island? It used to be called *Casa de los Cayos?*"

She stopped and gazed at me with that glass eye, scrutinizing, analyzing. Did I really expect someone to know about a place that had existed seventy years prior? "It might not be around anymore," I added with a shrug. "Never mind."

It was a long shot, but no harm in asking.

Syndia held onto the counter with both hands, vacant eyes wide. Judging from the way she looked at me—*finally* looked at me—I knew I'd hit a nerve. Her eyelids narrowed over her good eye. "Where did you hear that name?"

Don't tell her, a voice warned. She hadn't liked my question, and I almost wished I hadn't asked. I would ask someone else in town tomorrow. "Uh...a history article about Key West or something. Thanks. Have a good night."

She studied me, everything from my face to my purse containing Nana's ashes, all the way down to my feet. "This is *Casa de los Cayos*," she said. "At least it used to be."

FOUR

"How does it look?" Mom asked over the phone.

I'd called her to tell her the incredible news that I'd happened to stumble into the right place by total accident. I called from the privacy of my room, of course. Didn't think Syndia would take well to hearing that my family used to live in her hotel and what I presumed was also her house. She seemed annoyed enough as it was.

"It looks...desolate, to be honest," I told my mother.

Sadness streaked Mom's voice. "Is the moon sculpture still there?"

"I don't know. Where do I find that?"

"I don't know either. I'll find the pic of Mom and me as a baby in front of it," she said. "And text it to you later."

"Okay." We talked a little more then I hurried to hang up.

My room was adequate but old with its outdated furniture, and the lights in the bathroom didn't work when I flicked on the switch. Tomorrow, I'd inform Syndia, maybe ask if she could change me to another room. She'd probably be in bed by now and I was so tired, it didn't matter.

Even though it was late, I wanted to get at least one cursory look around the resort before going to bed. From what I'd seen so far, La Concha Inn was a collection of three houses, a centered main two-story building with a living room, dining room, office, and an atrium leading outside. Two houses of one story each flanked the main home, subdivided into three guest rooms. In the center of the backyard was a walled-in scant garden about twenty feet wide with a drizzly half-busted fountain in the center and a giant, creepy tree near the inlet. Enormous vine-root-things dropped from the tree's branches and sank into the ground, giving it the appearance of a massive animal chained by the neck and tethered to the ground.

The rest was too dark to see at this time of night. The whole property must've spanned an acre or so, bordered by long stretch of seawall in the back reaching from one end to the other. The humid August night smelled of salt and rotting coastal plants.

Which building used to be my grandmother's, I wondered? They all looked weathered enough to be original structures. Would anybody working here be old enough to remember? Syndia seemed to be in her fifties, her assistant in the office was even older, and my mom wouldn't remember. I couldn't ask Nana anymore, which burned me.

I headed out for a stroll.

Though it was almost 11 pm, I heard voices coming from the garden. There were other guests here? Why that shocked me, I didn't know, but it did. There they were, having beers in the lounge chairs. As I inched closer to them, I felt like I was sinking deeper and deeper into some land of the lost. The garden was overgrown with wild plants and weeds strangling anything that dared to stand out or be beautiful. The fountain trickled sadly. The gravel walkway had become overrun with stray grasses. Running my hand along the circular rock wall surrounding the fountain and garden area, I paused.

A chill ran through me. Granted, it was late at night and we were situated by the water, but a burst of cold air in the Florida summertime heat felt out of place. I pulled my hand away from the rock wall and moved closer to the people. An elderly couple in matching shorts and polo shirts sat in the extended lounge chairs along with a middle-aged couple about my mother's age. I felt better just knowing other life forms were staying here with me.

They quieted their conversation as I walked by. I waved to show I meant no harm and moved to the seawall overlooking the inlet. Here, I could appear like I was minding my own business while still overhearing their conversations, as they exchanged opinions about the establishment in muted whispers.

"How about you guys?" one woman asked.

"We'll be leaving in the morning. Not happy. Not happy at all, and..." I couldn't make out the entirety of what the wife was saying. "I don't even want to say it."

"She thinks there's ghosts in the rooms," her husband chimed in like a hero for vocalizing what she'd been too scared to say out loud. He chuckled condescendingly.

"Oh, really?" the other couple asked.

Yes, she said. Something about feeling like somebody was watching them in this very garden and last night in the guest room, it felt like a presence had crawled into bed with her.

"Well, at least someone did," the husband cracked, and the other husband cackled like that was the funniest joke ever.

I wanted to tell them that ghosts weren't real. They were fabrications of our minds, that the brain was a powerful organ. That they might even be a symptom of a brain disorder. When I was a kid, I swore ghosts followed me around, until I was diagnosed with cover obsessive compulsive disorder. And then, just like that, with a little pill, the ghosts disappeared. The only ones haunting me now were my own regrets.

I continued to listen with fascination.

"Did you hear about the tropical storm coming this way?"

In my shadowy corner of the garden, I faced them. Storm? I hadn't seen anything about a storm on the news, and the part of my brain that went into worry overdrive perked up at the news. The woman mentioned it could become a Category 1 storm by tomorrow, but it was too early to tell and anyway, it was still out wandering the Atlantic.

"It won't come this way," one husband said. "That's still days away; anything can happen, and from my experience, those things always cut right through the Caribbean and head to Texas."

"Oh, true, true," the other husband agreed. "We should be fine."

"When did you become a meteorologist, Roger?" one wife asked. I could almost see her eye roll in my head.

"It's always the poor countries that need most help after these storms," the other wife said. "I mean, look at Puerto Rico after Hurricane Maria. So devastating."

"Puerto Rico's not a country, hon. It's America."

"You know what I mean," she replied.

Was this true about the storm? Had I really come arrived to town on the worst week of the year? If worse came to worst, I could book a flight home, get out of the islands in time, couldn't I? *Oh, sure, along with thousands of other evacuees, Ellie.* Great, because my OCD needed more negative thoughts to obsess over.

No, everything would be fine, I told myself. One good thing about tropical storms over other natural disasters—you had days to prepare. You could see them coming miles away. Still, I wished I'd checked the weather sooner, or I wouldn't have come until hurricane season was over.

I felt stupid for being impulsive during that kitchen conversation with Mom when I'd agreed to bring Nana's ashes like some family heroine. Normally, I thought things through carefully. This time, it was like a voice inside my brain had made the decision for me. Regardless, I would enjoy my time here as long as I could.

After a few minutes of feeling the ocean breezes waft through the inlet, listening to the sounds of waves crashing below, I got hit with the tireds. It'd been a long-as-heck day, so I headed back to my room, making sure to take a full Zoloft and Ambien so I could get some sleep. I didn't want the native man visiting my dreams again tonight.

Harmless or not, he'd creeped me the hell out, and I was already creeped out enough as it was. Especially when I found Room 2's door wide open, as if someone had just been there, even though there was no one inside and I was sure I'd closed it myself.

"Hello?" I entered the room and scanned around.

Nobody was there, not in the bathroom or closets either. Maybe I hadn't closed the door all the way, or the latch was faulty and wouldn't shut right. Either way, I was perfectly safe and needed to stop obsessing. If only that wasn't so hardwired into my being.

I woke to the sounds of birds chirping and shuffling outside my window. I caught a flash of green. Wild parakeets? The sun filtered through the blinds, lending much-needed light to my room. The bad news was now I could see every crack, water stain, and ancient piece of furniture clearly. I focused on my phone instead.

My mother had texted while I'd slept. She'd sent the photo mentioned last night—a black-and-white faded image of a young and beautiful Nana holding my mother as a one-year-old. They stood in front of a rock sculpture in the shape of a quarter moon.

This is what it looks like, she'd texted. *Mom always mentioned this moon. Dad made it for her out of coquina.*

What the heck was coquina? Some type of rock, obviously. From the photo, it looked like the same rock used to make the garden wall, the seawall, and half the walls around this place. I had a lot to learn about Key West life. Maybe the innkeeper could answer a few questions for me. Would Nana's neighbors still be the owners of the inn? The neighbors she'd mentioned a few times who she swore hated her guts? I doubted it. If my grandmother had been eighty-eight when she died, then they were either just as old, way older, or dead.

If Syndia had recognized the name *Casa de los Cayos,* maybe she was part of the original family. I'd have to ask. I saved Mom's photo in my camera roll, got dressed, and headed out to see if I could locate the sculpture. How cool would it be if the thing still existed seventy years later?

By day, the garden didn't look any better. At least nightfall helped disguise how bad it was, but in full sunlight, the measly water dripping from the fountain was as depressing as the rusted cracks down either side of it. Most plants grew so wild, they lacked organization and made me feel I was staying in a jungle rather than a resort. The lounge chairs where the couples had sat talking last night were sun-faded with cracked plastic straps stretching across rusted metal frames.

The circular rock wall surrounding this center hub

looked like it'd been built over many years by different amateurs. The layers of porous rock were different colors, reminding me of all those charts showing layers of earth in science textbooks. Uneven craftsmanship. Not attractive in any way and depressing as hell. The only good thing about the yard was the majestic tree chained to the earth by its own choking roots. Even though it looked like a prisoner in its own space, it was still beautiful in a Frankenstein sort of way.

Banyan…

I looked around.

Had somebody said something?

A cold chill wrapped around me before wafting off, carried by the warm breezes. I shook it off, unnerved that I'd heard what sounded like someone talking nearby. Today *would've* been a good day to find a better resort to stay at, but now that I knew this was *Casa de los Cayos*, I had to stay. I'd come to spread my grandmother's ashes. I couldn't leave until I'd done that.

The closer I got to the inlet and ocean, the lighter I felt. Something about the salty air lifted the heaviness of the garden right off my shoulders. It made me sad to think that Nana's childhood home had fallen into ruins like this. By the property's edge, the water sparkled like diamonds underneath the sun. I thought about the best place to release her ashes, if to release them at all when I spotted it—the crescent moon sculpture.

Tucked away behind wild glossy fronds (were those bananas growing underneath?), the sculpture peeked out pathetically from under the foliage. This might've sounded crazy, but it almost seemed relieved to see me, as if it'd been waiting all this time for anybody to notice it hidden underneath the overgrowth.

I pulled up the photo Mom had texted me and held

my phone up to the sculpture. Same shape, same porous rock, same base, same view of the water behind it. My heart did a little victory dance. How could they let it get covered like this? It was one of the only beautiful things in this garden. I stood beside the sculpture and fired off a series of smiling selfies, then I took a few of the thing without my face.

Another chilly breeze whipped around me. It was a stifling ninety-five-degree heat out. It was strange, but then again, ocean air did bring cool breezes through. I just never realized how much. I texted the photo to my mother: *Look what I found!*

I felt so excited with my discovery that I postponed my plan to run out to Duval Street for sightseeing and spent time with the sculpture instead. I ran my hands over it—bumpy, raw, organic. So this was *coquina.* A quick online search told me it was a type of porous limestone harvested from the shores of Florida, used for building forts, seawalls, and sometimes foundations of homes. Apparently, it could be carved into anything, including quarter moons.

But all I cared about was that my grandfather had carved this particular piece. My own flesh and blood, the grandpa I never knew, had laid his hands all over this rock, toiled under the tropical sun to shape it. He'd fashioned this shape out of love for my grandma.

The only gifts I'd ever received from Zachary had been bought. Easy, whip-out-the-credit-card type stuff, the kind of present anyone could've bought at the last minute. Nothing like this. Nothing special.

"He must've really loved you, Nana," I said aloud, hoping my message would streak across the universe and reach her, wherever she was.

Studying the photos again, I noticed a few had

captured beams of light streaking across the moon, blocking its beauty. I deleted those then noticed something else—in the background of a few, depending on the angle, was a woman.

An old woman in a wheelchair.

Hunched over. Ancient.

I moved to the seawall for a better look.

She sat by the water on a lower level of the dock. I shielded my eyes from the glare, watching her. Vacant stare, mouth agape, older than even my nana, motionless as the boats floated along the inlet.

On a nearby bench, the woman from the office sat a while reading from a paperback. After a few minutes, she stood and stretched, placing her hands on the ancient woman's shoulders. "Come on, Miss Violet," she said in a Caribbean accent. She wiped the old woman's mouth and began wheeling her away. "Time for your nap, old girl."

FIVE

Something about the old crone unsettled me. Poor thing, catatonic and unresponsive, just hunched over in the wheelchair. Nana had always said if we had to wipe her chin or change her diaper, then she'd no longer want to be alive. Luckily, she hadn't been in that state for long. She'd left Earth on her own terms.

Combined with the resort's state of disrepair, it was no wonder business wasn't booming. And though I'd come to Key West to spread my grandmother's ashes, I'd also come to get away and relax. So I spent the day down on Duval Street, bar and store hopping, and it wasn't long before I'd sank back three margaritas at Hog's Breath Saloon with tourists who'd come off a cruise ship parked out in the ocean.

I must've made ten new friends while out, though I couldn't remember the names of any of them. One of them told me he was a ghost tour guide in town and showed me where the group departed every night, rain or shine. A woman about my age drank with her friends, celebrating her divorce, and upon finding out I'd recently broken up with my boyfriend, bought me my fourth margarita.

I was so smashed, I couldn't drive back to La Concha. Hell, I couldn't even find my car. I'd have to rideshare back then return for the rental tomorrow morning.

35

When I got back to the resort, I thanked my driver then entered through the front instead of the side guest entrance I'd seen this morning. Syndia happened to be at the front desk, so I stopped in to speak with her. "Hello, Ms. Duarte."

She stopped eating sunflower seeds long enough to grunt then look up at me through that freaky glass eye. "What."

What? Not *yes*, not *may I help you?* My goodness, this woman needed hospitality courses. I didn't let it bother me. "The light in my bathroom isn't working," I said, allowing her time to respond. No such a thing took place. "I was wondering if you could move me to another room."

"All I have is Room 3," she muttered going back to her sunflower seeds.

"Okay. Is there something wrong with Room 3?"

She looked at me as though I should know. Then, as if suddenly remembering I was the weird guest who'd mentioned *Casa de los Cayos* by name, the one new to town, she sighed. "We don't usually rent it out. It's old, but the lights and water work fine."

Why wouldn't she have rented it to me in the first place, then, instead of Room 2? "Works for me." I smiled to counter the feelings of negativity Syndia was emitting.

"Where did you say you were from again?" Her good eye narrowed. The glass one didn't move.

She should've known this from the info I'd given her at check-in, but I humored her anyway. "Boston."

"Are you the daughter of Mariel Drudge?"

Well, well.

Someone had spent some time digging. After my question about *Casa de los Cayos*, I shouldn't have been surprised she'd taken to investigating. It wasn't hard to track me or my mom down by name. We were both on social media and always linked as mother-daughter.

"I am, though it's Whitaker now," I said. "Not Drudge." Then, figuring since we were getting nosy with each other, I'd ask a question of my own. "Are you related to the family who runs the resort?"

"That side…" She pointed to the half where I was staying, "used to be my home when I was little, where my sisters and I grew up. When my grandparents passed away, we opened the inn on that half, where you're staying now, and moved to the other side of the compound." So, family house on left, guest rooms to the right—check.

"Your sisters live here, too?" I asked.

She took a while to answer, as though the question caused her physical pain. "They're in Miami." She ground the sunflower seeds between her teeth. "They only visit when they need something. My mother and I are the only ones left. Why are you here?"

Hostile, accusing tone. I swallowed and tried to ignore the feeling of pressure on my chest like I was unwanted here. "My grandmother passed away. She'd always talked about growing up in this place."

"Your grandmother being…?" Her question seemed more for her own confirmation. She already knew.

I indulged her anyway. "Leanne Drudge."

Syndia froze, dissecting eyes staring at me. Then, she suddenly remembered to breathe. I thought she would ask more questions, and we'd begin a dialogue about how our families knew each other, but she didn't pursue it. She reached into the drawer and pulled out another key. "Wait an hour for us to get it ready then bring back the other key after you've moved."

"I will. Thanks." Teetering off, I felt dread and

anguish all rolled into one come over me. Why would she have been offended to know who I was? And why did I feel like I wasn't welcome here?

My mother's apprehension came to mind when she'd told me she felt this placed was cursed, that Nana hadn't left Key West under the best of circumstances. I hated not knowing the whole story and hated myself even more for not getting it when I had the chance.

Walking through the garden at night brought out the worst of my OCD. Before I knew it, that oppressive feeling of doom I felt in the center hub enveloped me completely. I knew it was a symptom of my disorder, so I ignored it the best I could. Still, it was hard not to imagine every shadow as a person out to get me or every bug that flew past as a spooky orb of light.

Something was following me.

I stopped right then, sniffed the air, and looked around. Nobody. Alright, enough of this. I pulled up my phone, ordering more sertraline from the local pharmacy. I'd have to go without a pill tonight but could pick them up first thing in the morning.

A voice spoke near my ear. *Whore...*

"Excuse me?" I whirled around. "Who's there?"

I scanned the wild landscape but no one was around. God damn it. What was happening? I'd probably heard a guest speaking from one of the rooms or caught a sound byte carried by the water. *You're freaking out for no reason, Ellie.*

"Shit." I wiped my brow in the thick heat and headed to Room 2 to collect my things. Since Syndia had asked me to wait an hour, I took a few more minutes and searched up my grandmother, Leanne Drudge, just to see what came up. Nothing except the obituary we'd printed back home. I added "Key West" to the search, and this time, a PDF result came back. I clicked on it and found her name on a list of residents from 1940-1950 underneath Bill Drudge, my grandfather.

That was it. No other information, which was both a relief and a mild disappointment. Part of me had hoped her whole history would show up, so I wouldn't have to dig for answers or talk to Syndia again.

I took another minute to check the reviews of La Concha Inn on various sites. No surprise that it only had one star, and most of the reviewers said they would've given it zero had the website allowed it. Most of the reviewers also mentioned sensing an oppressive presence throughout the compound, and several wrote full paragraphs about the eerie things that had happened in their rooms, everything from cold spots to the sensation of being watched by unseen forces, to outright apparitions walking through the walls.

Yeah, okay. I laughed. More undiagnosed patients of hallucinogenic brain disorders.

No mentions of weird happenings in Room 3, though, so that was good.

I dragged my stuff to Room 3 and unlocked the room. Musty humidity seeped out, as the space seemed to exhale then draw its first breath in years. I clicked on the light switch, and a dirty yellow glow illuminated the space.

Syndia was right—it wasn't much, but it was better than Room 2 only because everything worked. Besides looking like another cheap hotel room, I could tell it'd also been used as storage, because of the brooms, mops, and buckets shoved inside the closet. The furniture was heavy teak, the kind of stuff you couldn't move once you'd set it down, and I wondered if any of it were original to the house. For all I knew, it could've been around for decades.

The art on the walls were crappy posters that had faded in the sunlight over the years, one of a parrot sitting on a branch and one of a footprint in the sand. Tacky. In the corner of the room, however, with an old lamp on it, was one, unique beautiful piece—a mosaic tile table.

Curious, I walked over to it and ran my fingers along the hand-placed tiles. Cobalt blue, light blue, and white gave the impression of ocean waves. An odd sensation came over me. Had I seen this table before? Of course not. I'd never been here. It looked handmade and had fallen several times judging from the cracked tiles on each corner.

A memory flitted through my mind all of a sudden— of me when I was about twenty, wearing a yellow sundress, happy like crazy that my boat captain fiancé had finally made it back from lobster trapping between Key West and Havana.

Only…I'd never lived in Key West or Havana before.

I'd never owned a yellow sundress before either, nor had a boat captain fiancé. Sinking onto the edge of the bed, I gripped my temples and tried to make sense of the thought. Where had that vision come from? I'd lived my entire life in Massachusetts. Those memories weren't mine.

Something shuffled out of the corner of my eye, but when I turned to face it head-on, nothing was there. Shadows, disembodied voices, a feeling of dread, hallucinations. All symptoms from my childhood days, though they usually affected me in sleep. All indicated deep stress infiltrating my psyche.

Then again, I'd had four margaritas today. That would make anyone hallucinate.

It was time—time to spread my grandmother's ashes then vacate. Split this place. Make like a tree and leaf. I might've felt different in the morning after doubling up on my medicine, but right now, I needed to get this over with. Grabbing my bag, I left the room, making a beeline for the unsettling garden. The moon sculpture would be the perfect place to honor her.

The ocean, I heard someone else's voice.

Nana?

She wanted me to release her into the ocean, I somehow instinctively *knew.*

But it couldn't have been her voice from beyond nor a gut feeling. It was just common sense. She'd lived by the sea. She'd lost her husband to the ocean. She would've wanted to be reunited with him. Fine, I'd spread half her remains at the sculpture and half at the water's edge. When I reached the rocky quarter moon, I placed my flat palm against it, waiting for some cue that it was time.

"Alright, let's do this." I couldn't wait any longer. My mother had been right. This place had a weird vibe about it. The only way to alleviate the discomfort would be to do what I came to do then go as quickly as possible. If that storm was heading anywhere near this place, it'd be the best choice anyway.

Opening the plastic bag containing the sandy granules that had once been my grandmother, I reached in and pulled out a handful of ashes and bits of bone. Did it feel odd holding her charred, decimated remains in my hand? Yes, but oddly, I felt close to her having this control, giving her soul—if there was such a thing—what it wanted.

I closed my eyes and called young Nana to mind. Beautiful, golden blond Leanne Drudge dancing in the breeze as a child living at *Casa de los Cayos,* pale green eyes staring out at the ocean, full breasts on a thin frame as a young woman, a sight for a weary sailor's sore eyes. Like coming home to pure love itself.

"Rest in peace forever, dear lady," I said, pushing my hand out and releasing her ashes all over the sculpture. I watched the particles swirl and dance on the breeze. I waited for, I didn't know, something magical to happen.

Nothing did.

I only felt sad and nostalgic and as far from peaceful as one might imagine. What had I expected? To feel fulfilled?

"Well, that's that." I began walking away from the sculpture when the wind picked up, or maybe I was imagining one. Not really a wind but not really a hallucination either, but *something* blew up from the inlet over the garden, rattling the plants and leaves. I watched as dust particles twirled in the light of a full moon above. It was probably the alcohol still coursing through me, but I also felt the ground shake just a bit, like a jolly giant from a fairy tale had taken one step before sitting down to rest.

Like the island itself had just coughed.

Taking the path to the seawall, I reached into my bag and pulled out another handful of Nana, holding out my arm and slowly releasing the bits and pieces. The grains fell from my hand like sand out of a funnel all over the dock, getting caught up in the cool ocean breezes, spiraling out to sea.

Finally, a certain peace came over me like I hadn't felt in the two days since I'd been here. Like coming home. Like being reunited with a loved one. Two things I'd never known.

But something new—I felt like I'd just unleashed hell for everyone else.

I wasn't alone. Down below on the dock was the old

woman again in her wheelchair, only she wasn't staring out to sea or space. Instead, her head was bent upwards, and she stared blankly, awkwardly at me at an unnatural angle, like her neck had been twisted to look up. Her mouth gaped open, vacant eyes forced out.

What the hell?

Was she dead?

To add insult to injury, I'd just sprinkled human remains over her by accident. Her nurse, the same woman from Syndia's office, sat on the nearby bench reading on an iPad. She hadn't noticed anything amiss, and I wasn't going to be the first to tell her the old woman seemed to have expired.

Catching my breath, I whirled around and bulleted through the garden, back the way I came. This place *was* cursed. *Shut up, Ellie, curses don't exist.* The real Ellie, the rational Ellie, wanted to stay and learn more about *Casa de los Cayos*, wanted to know more about Syndia and her family who'd purchased my grandmother's home. But before the night was over, she'd be dealing with the death of the woman in the wheelchair.

She deserved it.

A male voice this time. Nobody sat in the lounge chairs talking. No other guests whispered in the night from what I could tell. Who deserved it? The old woman? I couldn't wait to buy more Zoloft in the morning and start doubling up, doctor's orders be damned. I had to stop these voices hell bent on talking to me.

Cutting through the unkempt garden, an army of shadows followed me like they'd all woken up at once. I desperately wanted to escape them. I wanted to reach my room and lay down for the night. The banyan tree looked like it wanted to break free of its chains and chase me.

None of it made sense.

I needed sleep. I needed my meds. They'd suppress whatever this attack was on my brain. All I had to do was go to bed and wake up tomorrow, clear my mind of the weirdness. Then, maybe I could stay an extra day, finally relax, sip that lemonade I'd been dreaming of since Boston, then go home. Mission accomplished.

I reached my room and closed the door, relieved to be away from the garden.

And then I saw him standing in the corner—the native man from my dreams.

SIX

The moment my gaze connected with his, the man disappeared.

But I saw him—I know I did. Full body apparition. He'd worn nothing but a loincloth and a beaded red-and-white overlay on his shoulders. His hair had been picked up in a bun, and he'd held a spear. Sun-baked skin. Lots of details for a hallucination.

I didn't know what to think. I only knew I was exhausted as hell. And now, I'd have to sleep in the same room with a ghost. But ghosts didn't exist, or so I thought? They were manifestations of an overactive mind. If my own brain had fabricated him, then why this man in particular? A man I'd never seen before in my life? Was he someone I'd met long ago and forgotten?

He hadn't seemed menacing. More like a quiet observer, watching over me. I didn't get any sense of danger, but I didn't like it either. Maybe this was why they didn't rent out Room 3.

I opened the windows for fresh air, leaving the shutters closed with the slats open. I showered, changed into fresh T-shirt and undies, and climbed into the old creaky bed. Looking around, I could tell I was in somebody's former bedroom from the old armoire, old pine floors with chair scratches near the wall, and perfect view of the garden. If I narrowed my eyes just right, I could imagine myself watching the inlet, waiting for that fishing boat to come back, the one that carried my husband.

What the hell? I pressed my palms against my eyelids. What fishing boat? What husband?? I needed sleep. I needed my sanity back.

But neither came easy.

He told me not to worry, that everything would work out fine, I would see. I would see, because he'd meticulously planned this trip down to the last detail, and today was the day of its execution. He kissed me goodbye, and when he did, I felt it was the last time I'd ever see him. I wasn't sure how I knew, but I just knew.

The baby in my arms and I watched him go. He waved his hat, jumped into the fishing boat down by the pier, and away they went. "Come back to me," I whispered. "I can't live without you."

Then, the woman came.

Or rather, the creature next door.

She smoked something fierce and liked to watch me plant herbs in my garden from her yard. Sometimes she hung out the window, sometimes stood on her back porch. Soon you'll be husbandless, and I'll take your house. Like hell you will. My husband is working hard for us. He'll come through. The words seemed not to come from our mouths but from some ethereal place like watery echoes. Sure he will, honey, she said. Sure he will.

A little girl kneeled in the weeds, plucking them and putting them in a pile. "Can I get some water now?" she asked, exhaustion all over her face.

"It's 'may I have some water?' And when you're

46

done, girl. You just got started."
Wasn't sure who these people were, and yet...I
knew them deeply. Had seen them millions of times.
The man was the love of my life, and the woman
could've been a witch from the way she spoke to me
with hatred pouring from her soul. A bad witch
anyway, like the green-skinned ones only with pale
skin and curlers in her hair. The little girl, I had no
clue.
We're sorry to inform you, the policeman said.
He was lying straight to my face. How could he?
But your husband is dead.
Something about that statement made him randy.
An opportunity had opened up. He wanted into my
house. He wanted me for his own...

I blasted awake in the center of the bed, a sheen of
cold sweat breaking out over my entire body. Gasping, I
gripped the sheets and fought for air. I scanned the room.
I could almost see them standing there—the officer, the
husband, the horrible woman. How could she have been
so cold? I was a young woman with a baby, no threat to
her, yet she treated me like I was something to be feared.

"Wake up, wake up, you idiot..." I wasn't any of
those things.

I was Ellie Whitaker, unmarried, childless, and
twenty-six years old. And I'd been dreaming. I wasn't
dreaming as myself. I was dreaming as Nana.

Something had happened here. Something terrible,
but not to me.

Outside, a rogue wind blew through the center
courtyard, whistling and forcing open the shutters. For a
moment, I thought I saw my husband from the dream
looking in through the window—Nana's husband,

rather—my grandfather as a young man. Standing still, gaping wound across his neck, blood dripping down his sweaty chest.

His wide open eyes watched me through dirt-covered face. He wanted me to know. To see. Jesus Christ, I needed my meds. When I blinked him away, another figure appeared to replace him, that of a cat—a large, gray cat.

"Bacon," I gasped. "What the hell?" I took a moment to catch my breath.

Then, jumping out of bed, I went to the window and opened the shutters, petted the cat's head once before pushing him off the sill into the courtyard. He protested with a loud *mrwow*, and I closed the shutters, this time locking the clasp and the slats as well.

It'd been a dream, a nightmare. I knew this. My brain knew this. My scientific mind could conjure up fifty million explanations for these visions, yet deep in my soul, in my heart where sometimes the only things mattered, I knew that something bad had happened here. Something involving Syndia's family and mine.

My walk to the pharmacy helped clear my mind.

The moment I paid for the Zoloft, I ripped open the package and swallowed back two whole ones. Then I made a note in my phone planner to make an appointment to have my dosage adjusted. My OCD had been under control until Zachary, until the night my grandmother fell into her coma. Since then, my repressed issues had all decided to come to the surface.

Great timing.

As I rounded the street corner back to La Concha Inn under light rain, I slowed down. An ambulance was parked out front, as two paramedics wheeled a covered body into the back. Off to the side, Syndia stood stiff with a tissue at her mouth, her eyes red and glistening. If the woman had looked gaunt and frail when I first met her, she looked ten times worse now. The old woman's nurse stood behind her, sporting a tight-lipped grimace.

"Is everything okay?" I walked through the open gate.

Syndia stared straight ahead. "My mother. She passed away late last night."

"Oh, I'm so terribly sorry." So, that had been her mother.

"Are you?" She cast a hurt gaze at me.

"Excuse me?"

"Are you sorry? You shouldn't say things like that unless you mean them." She held my gaze for a few hateful seconds more then stomped up the steps and entered the house. The two paramedics gave me sympathetic looks.

I felt like I'd been slapped, like I was culpable for what had transpired here. Why did I feel guilty when I hadn't done anything wrong? The woman had been practically a thousand years old, for hell's sake. I mean, I felt bad for Syndia, sure, but it was her time to go anyway. My being here had nothing to do with it.

"People say weird things when they're in pain," one of the paramedics said to me.

I nodded and moved past them. Unable to help myself, I glanced back at the stretcher inside the ambulance. The old woman lay underneath the white sheet, her filmy eyes vacant, her cracked mouth open, saliva drying up. She wheezed, emitting gases and bodily fluids. I gasped, wondering how the hell I could see all that if she was covered.

The ambulance doors closed.

I moved past the woman's nurse, noting the worry on

her face and entered the house, hoping to return to my room where I could decide what to do—whether to leave town or stay. Then I saw the other four guests gathered around the dining table watching TV. Amid their unappetizing muffins and bowls of cheap cereal, they chattered as they watched a satellite image of a storm system.

A big-ass storm system.

The weatherman, in his snazzy suit, buzzed about the screen. "Here you see Tropical Storm Mara blazing a trail through the Turks and Caicos Islands, traveling at a speed of twenty-five miles per hour…"

I walked into the dining room and leaned against the wall to listen.

"The bad news for us here in the Florida Keys is that we're close to receiving the dreaded National Hurricane Center Tropical Storm Warning, but the good news is that storms traveling this quickly tend to be over soon. Last thing we want is a slow-moving storm that dumps rain on us for days."

"A hit and run," one guest mumbled.

Another couple stood, the curly-haired wife with the manicured nails picking up her purse and sunglasses. "We need to get going before traffic gets bad. Well, hope you all get out safely. It was great meeting you," she said to the other couple then headed down the corridor.

"What about us? What do we do?" the other wife asked her husband.

"Let's see what the weatherman says. It might not come."

"Even if it doesn't come this way," I chimed in shyly. "We'll still get those outer feeder bands the weather man was talking about and lots of rain. See them?" I pointed to the swirly outer cloud bands on the satellite image.

"So much for our fun-in-the-sun, tropical vacation!" The husband stood and stretched. "Alright, dear, let's pack this puppy up and take it home. What about you?" he asked me. "You staying?"

"Not sure. I'll check flights out from Key West and decide."

"They're all cancelled," the man said. "We just heard it on the news. All local flights. Your best bet is to drive to Miami and fly from there, if you get out in time. What I'm worried about is the bumper-to-bumper traffic. By the time we make it, the area's under a hurricane warning."

"Right," I said. "I'll have to consider all options." I'd been through bad Nor'easters before, but not a tropical storm. What was the difference besides rain instead of snow? Wasn't it just a matter of hunkering indoors until it passed?

"Well, good luck to you."

"Thanks, you too."

The couple left, just as Bacon jumped onto the table to take scraps of what they'd left behind. As my gaze followed them out of the dining area, it landed on a fireplace in the living room. Above the mantel was a gilded shadow box, something shiny glinting inside.

Bacon rubbed against my leg, asking for more food.

"I don't have anything, buddy," I told him. Checking to see if Syndia was anywhere in sight, I reached into the muffin basket, ripped off a chunk of dry muffin and set it on the floor. Bacon sniffed it but turned up his nose. "Sorry, then. Go kill a mouse or something."

The cat stalked into the living room and stood underneath the mantel looking back at me, almost as if saying, *Come on, come look at this.* He seemed very proud of this room, so I walked over and peered into the shadow box on the mantel. A photo of three gold, round pieces topped a frame article from the *Key West Gazette*. Below it was dated Labor Day, 1951.

The basic gist was this: Key West resident, Robert McCardle, had found a bag of gold doubloons during his shift piloting the Havana Ferry back from Cuba. The bag had mysteriously appeared on the ferry before which he'd dutifully turned it into the police. As no one had come to claim it, the police let him keep the Spanish gold coins. As a result, Robert McCardle purchased the adjacent home next to his to accommodate his expanding family, but sadly, the man died unexpectedly from a massive heart attack the very next year.

My heartbeat picked up. Wait.

Robert McCardle had found treasure in 1951? But I thought my grandfather had been the treasure hunter and fisherman on this property. Shouldn't it say Bill Drudge? It was like my family's name had been erased from history.

"Them only the tip of the iceberg."

I whirled around. Miss Violet's nurse stood there, arms stiff by her side. Bacon hissed at her.

"Hi." I extended my hand. "I'm Ellie."

She took my hand. "Nottie."

"Nice to meet you. What do you mean these are only the tip of the iceberg?"

She stared at the shadow box. "Rumor say there's a lot more gold than that one bag McCardle found." She glanced around nervously, wringing her hands. "He purchased the house next door, you know—your grandmother's house."

"Right, that's what I've heard. Is Room 3 part of her original house?"

The woman wouldn't answer me. "They say he hid

the rest so nobody would attack him for it," she whispered. "Robert McCardle did."

Attack, or accuse? "Who would attack him for it?" I asked, trying to imagine a 1950s fisherman hiding his treasure in the house like a paranoid madman.

"Treasure hunters, pirates..."

"Pirates?" I half-laughed. What century were we living in?

"Not the peg leg kind with the feathered hats, but yes," Nottie assured me. "Anyone looking to steal your loot around here is a pirate, you know."

"Got it." I nodded.

"Nottie." The voice was stern and sudden. We turned to find Syndia rounding the coffee table making a slow descent on the poor nurse. "That's enough. You can go now." Her frown told me my informant wasn't supposed to tell me any of that.

"Sorry, Ms. Duarte." Nottie took off faster than a cat burglar under the sudden beam of a cop's flashlight.

Syndia's glassy gaze seemed to accuse me of something I couldn't decipher. "Yes, pirates are a common thing here in the islands. People stealing what's not *theirs*."

Did she think I was here to take something? I didn't believe the silly little story on the fireplace mantel anymore than I believed some hotels bragged about being haunted, just to attract visitors. Talk of pirates and hidden treasure was a lure for tourists seeking adventure. Especially coming from an establishment that needed more business such as this one.

Syndia already knew I'd heard Nottie's version so I went with it. "Wouldn't McCardle have told his wife where he hid the rest?" I asked. "I mean, why would he keep such important info to himself?"

"Men didn't confide in their wives in those days. Her role was to run the house, not the finances. Besides, he became paranoid after finding the gold. He always felt that someone would take what was rightfully his."

Sounded like guilt to me. A bag of gold suddenly showed up on your ferry and you got to take it home, rich as butter pie? Reminded me of the story of Sarah Winchester, perpetually afraid that the ghosts of those killed by her family's famous Winchester rifles would haunt her, so she built a home with endless rooms, doors, windows, walls, and staircases.

In this case, Robert McCardle had hid his treasure to keep the bad men away.

"Anyway, it's none of your concern. Can I help you with something else, Miss Whitaker?" Her eye stared at me with lifeless intensity.

"So you're telling me this...treasure...is still in the house somewhere?" I couldn't believe what I was hearing. She wouldn't answer, so I looked back at the shadow box, noticing now a brass plaque at the top. Printed on it—*La Concha's Very Own Legend.*

"You better get on the road, Miss Whitaker." Syndia stared at me. On the TV behind her, the 11 o'clock hurricane advisory had just begun, and the weatherman's excitement had just risen a notch. "That tropical storm that's coming? Just turned into a Category 1."

SEVEN

Something didn't add up.

A *lot* didn't add up.

First, how would a bunch of gold just show up on a busy ferry, and only the captain saw it? Wouldn't he have been the most busy person on the vessel? Wouldn't a random passenger have found it first? Second, why would the police have let McCardle keep the gold? Did they take a nice cut of the proceeds for being so generous? Third, if McCardle's family, my grandmother's neighbors, did become rich over all this, why was the place falling apart? Money like that would've lasted a nice long time, wouldn't it?

I didn't know. Like I said, didn't add up.

Apparently, their luck had run out, starting with McCardle's heart attack the following year.

If the story Nottie told me had been fabricated to lure in customers, then why wouldn't Syndia make a bigger deal of it? Why not bill their establishment as one big treasure hunter's wet dream come true? Promote the heck out of the place as a pirate's cove. I realized, suddenly, that was why there were old statues of a pirate out front. And a parrot. And a shell.

They had tried doing just that, but nobody fell for themed Florida hotels anymore. They were relics of the past. Did Syndia seriously think I was here to steal her gold? Enough to ask me if I was Mariel Drudge's daughter, enough to turn pale upon learning who I was and mentioning my grandmother's home by name?

Come on, seriously.

Even if there *were* gold buried somewhere on this compound, how the hell would I find it? Sure, let me just whip out my psychic sledgehammer and tear the place apart. But there were more pressing issues to consider at the moment, and that was whether or not to go with a storm a-comin'.

I took a walk around the compound, checking out areas I hadn't yet seen. Where the other couples were staying, for example, the building looked newer but not renovated. I was hoping to assess how structurally sound the buildings were in the event I decided to stay, but then my mother Face-Time'd me.

"How did I know you'd be calling me today?" I smiled into the phone.

One look at her face, and I knew she was in Mom mode. "Ellie, you need to come back to Boston. There's a storm headed that way."

"It's just a tropical storm. It's not a massive hurricane."

"Ellie, it's a Category 1 storm, and might I remind you you're on a tiny island?"

"So?"

"So, all the ocean needs to do is surge up a few feet, and you'll be underwater."

I hadn't considered the storm surge, but from where I'd stood at the dock's railing, the water level was way below the foundation of this area. It wasn't like the house was on a beach. "You know, this place might not look much from the outside, but I feel like it's safe."

"You can't know that, Ellie," Mom argued. "You're

not a hurricane code expert. Just...get on a plane and come home, please. Listen to your mother for once."

I debated whether or not to tell her what was going on here. The stuff I was finding out. Sometimes, when I involved my mother in my decision-making, she made things worse by telling me her "gut" feelings. "There hasn't been a mandatory evacuation yet," I said. "If there is, then I'll definitely leave."

"You're being stubborn. I just don't get why," my mother said, pinching the bridge of her nose.

"Mom, why did you say that Nana had to sell this house again?"

"She couldn't afford to keep it. A single mother raising a small child in the fifties, Ellie. Single mothers didn't own houses in those times unless they'd been left with a lot of money or life insurance, and my grandfather was a poor fisherman. He didn't make sure she was taken care of in the event of his death. He should've used his free time to find a second job instead of go treasure hunting." She scoffed. "Didn't find shit anyway."

But then Robert McCardle came home with treasure, while my grandfather was declared dead, boating accident.

It wasn't no accident, Nana's voice rang through my mind.

You'll be husbandless. The neighbor's words from my time travel dream snaked into my mind. *And then I'll take your house.*

I smelled cigarette smoke. I stopped in the corridor and stared ahead at a tangled mess of wild plants. Nobody was there. No smokers, though smoke could've wafted in from anywhere.

Whore...

Who the hell kept calling me that?

"What is it, Ellie?" Mom asked. "You look like you've

seen a ghost."

I kept staring ahead. My mind wandered. "You know I don't believe in that."

"You did when you were little, before we found out what was really going on. Ellie, are you taking your medicine?" It could've been normal maternal concern, but I felt like there was something she wasn't telling me.

"I've been doubling up."

"Good."

"Why do you ask?" I pushed through a section of the plants and stepped deep into the brush. Obsessed. Compulsive. "What would happen if I stopped taking them? It's been a while, so I kind of forgot."

"Your obsessions take over. Negative thoughts attack, and you'll blame it on yourself. You'll hallucinate in your sleep, sometimes out of sleep."

"Are you sure that's all? Is that why I started taking them?" I asked, plants scraping and scratching at my pale arms. What if they hadn't been hallucinations? What if they'd been real visions of real things and all this time I'd been suppressing them?

"Well, yes. Where are you going? What's with all those plants?"

My eyes fell on something rustling in the bushes. "I was just checking something. Thought I saw a cat," I lied. Whatever it was, it made the plants move around like a dinosaur wading through grass.

"Okay, well, look for flights then let me know what you find."

"Okay, Mom."

"Even if you have to drive out of Florida, Ellie. We can get you a flight from Atlanta or something. Just get out of Key West."

"Okay, I'll call you later." I hung up without saying

goodbye.

There was no way I was leaving. Too many questions burned my mind, and the same gut feeling that kept my mother at bay from this place lured *me* in deeper. Questions like, what the hell was walking through the grass? I parted the leaves of a massive bush, expecting to see a cat or a raccoon and froze. My heart stopped. There in the grass was a person lying on the ground. A man in a fine-tailored suit covered in dark red blood. Was he real? What was he doing here? I suppressed the urge to throw up, though my mouth filled with warm saliva. Suddenly, it was like an invisible pair of hands lifted the man's legs up and began dragging him through the grass, a little bit at a time with clear effort.

I meant to scream. I needed to, but I was paralyzed. The sound caught in my throat.

"Why are you here, Miss Whitaker?"

I whirled around, my heart pounding through my ribcage. Jesus Christ, why did this woman keep sneaking up on me? Did she not see the dead body being dragged through her property? I looked back again to point it out, but the man was gone. Nothing there but plants and weeds.

"Holy shit…" I grunted out. "Can you…not do that, please? Not come up behind me like that?" I scoffed and backed out of the foliage.

"Answer my question. Why did you come here?"

I snapped. "That's not your business, but since you seem so suspicious of me, I came to spread my grandmother's ashes. Happy now?" I dropped my hands at my sides. "This might be your home today, but my grandma lived here a long time ago. She loved this place with all her heart. My mother was *born* here. Do you understand, Ms. Duarte?"

Syndia stared at me with those mistrustful eyes, saying nothing.

"You don't," I said. "Because you didn't spend your entire life hearing your grandma talk about a place she could never return to. You didn't hear the pain in her voice over losing it. That name...*Casa de los Cayos*...I must've heard it a thousand times growing up. Do you know what it means to me to be here?"

"You're not entitled to anything on this property."

"I know that. For shit's sake, stop saying that."

"Spreading ashes takes a second. You've stayed longer than that. You're curious. You're snooping around my house. I need you to leave, Miss Whitaker."

Was she serious?

I noted the grave expression on her face. She was damn serious and hella crazy too. However, she'd also just lost her mother. "Ms. Duarte, if you think I'm here to find your missing treasure, you need to know that I don't care about your fictitious gold. What I care about is truth. I only want to know what happened to my family. What really happened."

"You'll never know what happened," Syndia said carefully. "None of us ever will. Our grandparents are gone, and with them...their secrets."

She was right about that.

But if I left now, I'd never have the chance to find out.

I came to connect and connect I would. Storm or no storm, I had to find out what happened here in 1951, why my grandmother carried so much hurt in her heart, why my mother felt a darkness here she couldn't face. Why a bleeding, well-dressed man had been dragged through the trees before my very eyes.

EIGHT

One moment, short gusts of wind were pushing sheets of rain right onto the window panes, and the next, the sun shone brightly like your average happy day. This was the calm before the storm. Hurricane Mara was headed up Cuba in the next two days then would cut right up the middle of the Florida Keys.

At least that was what the Cone of Death suggested on TV.

I spent a good amount of time on my phone checking flights and the traffic situation, just so I could tell my mother that I'd tried. I also did a fair amount of research on the probability of surviving a Category 1 hurricane. According to the articles I read, very few locals ever evacuated the Keys unless a Category 3 or higher was on the way. Tropical storms and Cat 1 storms were playthings to most Florida folks.

Part of me actually looked forward to bearing the brunt of the angry seas.

Part of me also contained the DNA of a diehard sailor.

And just for shits and grins, I researched whether or not Syndia Duarte could kick me out just because she wanted to. Apparently not, as this was my shelter from the storm but also a registered place of business and I'd done nothing to disrupt the peace.

During one of the sunny breaks between rain bands, I heard a car engine outside and peeked through the blinds to see her leaving. It must've been difficult having to run a place of business and prepare for a storm while also dealing with your mother's death. I exhaled, thankful I didn't have to deal with her for at least a little while.

A scratch at my door gave me pause. Slowly, I turned and stared at it. The noise did not repeat itself. Heading over, I opened it only to find a fallen dried palm frond on the ground getting whisked away by a sudden breeze. The new levels of humidity startled me. Moisture stuck to my skin like a thick layer of steam that wished to become a sweater.

Just as I was about to close the door, Bacon meowed his presence and rubbed up against my legs. I could've kicked him out, but what would've been the point? He seemed to like me better than his owner and besides, I could've used the company.

"Hey, buddy. I don't have food." I laughed. "I don't have any bacon for you, Bacon."

The cat waited at the door while staring into the room with big golden eyes. I wondered if he could sense the native man who had appeared here yesterday. If he could, he certainly wasn't afraid of him and strutted into the room anyway. After walking around nonchalantly, examining my bags, my shoes, and my towel on the floor, Bacon entered the bathroom nook and disappeared into a closet.

I followed him.

Behind a modern built-in strongbox, the kind that came with most hotel rooms, was a four-inch space. And behind that four-inch space in the wall was a hole. A carved out hole like someone had taken a crude little saw and made it by hand. Bacon squeezed into the space. A moment later, he curled up by the cat-sized mouse hole and began purring.

This cat had a hideout in this room? "What are you doing in there, bud?" I got on my hands and knees. The cold terrazzo floors were dusty and dirtied my hands.

I reached into the hole and ran my fingers through his thick fur. He purred even louder when my fingers connected with the space between his ears. Jealous that he could see where he was and I couldn't, I grabbed my phone and fit it into his crawl space, snapping several shots in different directions.

Most of the pics were too close and too muddy to show anything, but one showed a rectangular outline on the wall and right at the edge was a small golden lock. Bacon blinked his green eyes at me like a Mona Lisa smile.

"What are you guarding, Bacon?"

I reached into the hole until my fingertips were touching the lock. It was a small lock, like the kind used on suitcases long ago, and when I tugged on it, it didn't budge.

"Be right back," I told the cat and left the room. I was pretty sure I was alone at La Concha Inn, that all the guests had left. Even Nottie was nowhere to be found. Nobody would care if I tested all the doors to see if any were used as a utility closet.

I found what I was looking for by the dining room. A thin closet door revealed a storage unit for cleaning solutions, mops, packages of napkins, take-home containers, a long clear hose with dried brown gunk in it, and shelves holding several basic tools. Grabbing a hammer and pliers, not sure which would work best, I closed the closet and ran back to my room.

Bacon was already outside, looking for me. La

Concha Inn's very own watch-cat. "What? I was coming back," I told him. Reentering the room, he followed me inside and stood like a sentinel nearby as I laid down on the floor in the closet and reached into the hole as best as I could with the hammer.

Smacking the lock a few times didn't help, so I used the pliers to grip the tiny lock then twist and twist until the weak, old metal broke free. I pulled open the small compartment and hesitated. Using the camera on my phone again, I took a few photos of the inside of the space.

A cold hand grabbed mine.

I shrieked and yanked my hand back, smacking the phone against the wall. What the hell was that? I waited a few feet back, sweat pouring from my temples, stomach in my throat, waiting for the hand to come out of the hole. "Who is that?" I asked. "Who's in there?"

Nobody replied.

My phone had a crack running through the middle of the screen now. Great. With the video camera on, I pushed it ever so slowly toward the hole again. Once it reached the edge of the hole, I lifted it and moved it side to side, scanning for any unseen presences, but it was hard to do with my hand trembling.

"Somebody there?" I asked again.

The air felt charged with energy. I wanted to lie down and peer into the hole with my naked eye but hesitated. Had the hand been real or another one of my visions?

I pulled the phone back and saw I hadn't captured any significant images of the wall's interior space. Part of me warned to end this right here, but part of me—the stubborn part my mother knew well—needed to see what was in that locked space.

Come on, Ellie. You can do this.

Closing my eyes, I decided to risk it again. Hallucinations couldn't hurt me, and if I kept my eyes closed, I didn't have to see them. Hopefully, I wouldn't feel them either. My fingers felt around the mustiness until they brushed against some papers.

Reaching in, I pulled the stack of small papers out only to find that they weren't papers at all but photographs. Old black-and-white photos. Scrambling to my feet, I peered at them with shaking hands. What I saw, photo after photo, would've been considered risqué at the time. Hell, they were pretty risqué even now. Boudoir photos of a woman. A beautiful woman. On her knees, on the edge of a sofa, breasts bared, legs tightly fused together. I guessed one might call them tasteful.

But the more I shuffled through them, the more I realized that the naked woman in black garter and stockings and heels and pearls, wearing a sexy smile and having a fun time was my very own grandmother.

Those eyes, those cheekbones, that turned up smile.

Bacon meowed.

"No, you may not see these. Oh, whatever." I crouched and showed the images to the cat who only wanted to rub his saliva-smeared cheek on them. I pulled them back before he could damage them. "You led me right to them," I said. "More evidence of the woman I loved. Thank you, buddy."

On the back was old handwriting, the kind of cursive you never saw anymore. Angled, scripty, with long loops. *Leanne, 1949.* My nana would've been nineteen in these. On the opposite corner of the photo was my own grandmother's handwriting: *To my dearest Bill, so you'll always have a thrill.*

Funny, Nana. Very cute.

I smiled so hard, my cheeks hurt. Then, I cried.

Because what were the chances of finding a face I loved hidden in these walls? Did the McCardles or Duartes know this was here?

I ran back to the hole in the wall to see what else I could discover, even at the risk of another hand grabbing me, but found nothing. The rest of the space disappeared into emptiness. So, my grandfather had a hiding spot for his nudie pics. Of my grandmother! And the hiding spot was still there after all these years. In fact, this whole room vibrated with a special frequency altogether.

Could this have been my grandparents' bedroom? It would explain the secret hiding spot and maybe the mosaic table that wasn't part of the usual hotel repertoire of furniture.

My mind whirled with the possibilities. I wanted to call my mom right away and show her what I'd found, but I could already hear the incessant questions. I'd work better if she knew nothing.

As I slid my hand back away from the secret compartment, my skin brushed against something taped to the back of the safe. I pulled at the masking tape. A tarnished brass key fell into my hand.

It wouldn't fit into the safe that was too modern. I checked the room to see if any of the furniture pieces required a key, but none did. Dropping it into my purse for safekeeping, I lay myself back against the pillow and stared at my grandmother's photos again. I loved that she felt carefree enough to pose like this. I loved that they'd been done for her husband. My grandparents' relationship was serious goals.

No wonder she'd missed him so much. She'd never even remarried.

It made me angry that Nana had to sell her home. Made me angry that other people moved in and took over. That someone else had found the treasure that my grandfather had tried so hard to find for himself and Nana.

I closed my eyes and tried to see them again. Maybe they would come to me in another dream and I'd again wear a yellow sundress and see my life through Nana's eyes. Instead, I listened to the next feeder band swish against the window panes and fell asleep from mental exhaustion.

The native man tugged at my feet.

He wanted me out of bed. I knew I was dreaming, but it felt real. Lucid. The wind outside picked up, but when I followed him past the door to Room 3, things were not the same. It was Florida alright, but Florida many years ago before it'd earned a Spanish name. No buildings, no cars, no palm trees.

Just beach and palmetto plants and abodes made out of sticks and dry fronds. Chickees, the man told me. This was his village. These were his people.

I looked around and saw many of them—men, women, children, old ones, babies.

They worked together in harmony. The men speared their fish just a few feet into the water and the women cleaned the fish and prepared them for meals. The children helped too, though several of them chased each other around the beach, ignoring their responsibilities. Fire gave the air a scent of sweet smokiness, and I felt like I'd been here before a long time ago.

This is my home, he told me. It wasn't English.

It wasn't any language I recognized, yet I understood him without him uttering a word. It was my home too, many years ago, before the Europeans. His face sagged when he pointed this out to me, and my basic knowledge of this land's history told me why. But this dream wasn't about history, nor was it about what they were doing in his village.

It was about the fire.

He pointed to it and told me that the women were using it to send messages to the sky gods. They'd burn the herbs and cast their intentions, focusing clearly on what they wanted, releasing their wishes into the ether. I could do it, too, but my mind was focused on the mathematical. The logical.

I didn't know what to tell him.

This wasn't my world and these weren't my practices.

He told me they were and always had been.

Then he disappeared, leaving me in the current day garden, feeling like my life had been empty until now but was ready to be filled.

When I woke up, I had a hard time remembering where I was. Disorientation hit me like a box truck, but then I saw the shutters. They'd been blown open. Cigarette smoke filled my room, even though I wasn't a smoker. Maybe one of the other guests were outside smoking?

I was about to get up and close the windows when the sheets were suddenly torn off the bed. By themselves. Just flew and landed on the floor in a heap. I stood there, shaking, not knowing what the hell to do. Visions were one thing, but visions didn't tear sheets off your bed. Fine, it was perhaps-maybe-possibly possible that ghosts existed. And I had an idea of who'd just been here, who'd come to harass me.

The woman next door who smoked. My grandmother's neighbor from long ago.

NINE

I spent the rest of the day trying to make sense of what was happening. Between my dreams, the photos I'd found, the visions, smells, and things I'd seen, plus Syndia's crazy talk about treasure, I felt rationality slipping away from me.

I also refreshed the National Hurricane Center's website often trying to keep up with everything going on in the earthly world, too. Hurricane Mara headed this way but wouldn't arrive for another day and a half or so. The on-and-off rain had turned into beautiful skies, which one weather lady on TV said was "God's way of giving us time to prepare."

What if we didn't believe in God?

I'd forgotten all about the rental car. It'd probably been towed by now, and I'd have to face a fee. Reportedly, traffic out of the Keys was stop-and-go, and those staying behind were out buying supplies, clearing store shelves of water, milk, bread, and canned goods. Traffic along Roosevelt had increased, and trucks drove by hauling plywood and piles of sand. Everywhere, people helped each other, and it prompted me to go see Syndia, ask if she needed to do anything to prepare.

I followed the garden path down to the main building and entered. The TV with the same weather station was on again, and I heard sniffling sounds coming from the front desk. Syndia sat there, head bowed at her desk.

"Do you need help preparing or anything?" I asked, then realized I should've coughed before sneaking up on her. Not that she ever did the same when sneaking up on me.

She looked up with tears in her eyes. "We've been bringing things in. You can help if you like." I felt bad for her and her situation, but something told me I shouldn't ask about it. I was sure I'd get blamed for it anyway.

"What about shutters?" I looked around. "I don't see any. Isn't that of utmost importance?"

"Utmost importance to me is if you could leave, Whitaker," she sneered, a hard bite in her voice. *Ouch.* "It's hard enough preparing for a storm with a guest like you here. I would kick you out, but by law, I have to provide shelter."

"I'm sorry. I only want to learn more about my grandparents. It's only fair, since they lived on half your property once."

"Well, you picked the wrong week to come. My mother is at a funeral home about to be embalmed, I'm trying to figure out how to pay for her funeral *and* bills if this storm hits…" Her voice built a crescendo as she went on. "And to make it all worse, you're playing detective when my stress is through the roof!" Her jaw clenched tight.

I swallowed. "I only asked if I could help."

"You could help by leaving." She gritted through her yellowed teeth.

"I don't think I can do that." When would I have another chance to come back? What if she sold the inn and turned it back into a private home? Then, I'd never have the same opportunity again.

"Well, I'm fresh out of information to give you." She

scoffed, exasperated. "What more do you want from me?"

"I want to know why my grandmother was forced to leave when she loved it here."

"She couldn't pay her mortgage. Simple as that. Why can't you let it lie?"

"Because I don't believe that," I said to my own surprise. What was I saying? That I suspected foul play, and here I was telling the very descendant of those who may have caused my grandmother harm? I needed to quit while I was ahead.

"What do you believe then?" A challenging look crossed her face.

I didn't have much to go on, only hunches, gut feelings, the sort of stuff I made fun of my own mother for having. No facts, only photos of my grandmother young, naked, and happy, and hallucinations by the dozens.

"I believe the truth always comes out," I said. "I'm sorry about your mother. It must be difficult what you're going through." And then I stepped out of the front desk and called a Lyft driver for one more trip downtown, hoping to find answers before it was time to hunker down for Mara.

I needed a historian or a time machine to help me through this.

Or both.

The Key West Historic Society had closed for the day "until further notice" and the people at the Hemingway Home were kind enough to let me in, though busy collecting their fifty resident six-toed cats (all descendants of Hemingway's original polydactyl kitty) in preparation for the storm.

I asked one guide there if he knew anything about *Casa de los Cayos* or the history behind La Concha Inn, and he simply shrugged and said that the resort was more full of ghost tales and speculation than actual history. I would be better off talking to Luis Gallardo at Sunset Spooks Ghost Tours, the agitated middle-aged man told me.

I'd heard that name before. In fact…

I reached into my purse and found the business card still there. I'd met Luis—at least I thought that was his name—while out drinking the other night. He'd told me where to meet for the tour, if I was ever interested. He'd said it went on every night, rain or shine.

So I headed that way, stopping first to find my rental car. Sure enough, it was missing, and I jotted down a note on my phone to call the company tomorrow about it. Maybe I could claim storm traffic for my inability to reach it.

I stood on the corner of Duval and Caroline Streets. Nobody was there. It was 8:30 and getting dark fast, as the next rain band started coming in softly. It'd be silly for anyone to conduct a ghost tour on a night like this, I thought, but then down the sidewalk, illuminated from behind by vendor floodlights, was the silhouette of a medium-build man in jeans and straw hat. A cigar stuck out the side of his mouth, unlit.

"Well, well, well…" He clapped his hands once, rubbed them together. He had a charming accent to match his Cuban shirt, the kind of linen shirt they sold in many shops along Duval Street with vertical stripes and pockets at the breast. "Every time I think no one will show up, there's always one adventure-seeker. Like walking in cemeteries in the rain, do you?"

I smiled. "Not exactly."

He arrived to where I stood and stuck out his hand.

"Name's Luis. And you look familiar."

I took his hand. "We met last week. Ellie."

"Ah, sí. Ellie from Boston." He smiled an easygoing grin. "I remember you. Are you a believer or non-believer?" he asked, wiggling his jolly eyebrows. "Of ghosts, of course. I always like to ask my guests."

"I'm not sure." I was surprised I hadn't just said non-believer straight-out.

"A healthy skeptic then." He chuckled, patting my shoulder. "I like that. And don't worry, I won't try to convince you that ghosts exists. I know they do and that's all that matters." He winked. "The evidence I'll show you during tonight's tour is all real. All photographic taken by our own guests, and a few EVPs—"

"Actually, Luis," I interrupted him. "Since I'm the only one here, I was wondering if I could just ask you some questions."

"So you're not going to make me do my whole song and dance?" he said, somewhat relieved. Holding up his palms, he tested the rainfall. "Good, because I just showered and wasn't looking forward to getting wet again. Want to go grab a drink?"

"Maybe coffee, if that's alright." I couldn't afford getting sloshed again. The effect could be deadly on my sanity.

Luis was more than happy to take me to the nearest coffee shop, which looked like it was about to close, but he knew the owners, so they let us stay. As we grabbed a table by the window, the harried staff worked to close the place up for the night. Outside, Duval Street looked eerie as locals boarded up their shop windows.

"Why haven't you left town like all the other tourists?" Luis asked. "I mean, don't get me wrong, the City of Key West thanks you." He chuckled.

"I came here for a mini-vacation that turned into a personal mission," I said. I didn't give him the details of how spreading my grandmother's ashes had turned into fighting for her legacy.

The server delivered our coffees, mine, creamy and frothy, in a tall glass and his, dark and strong, in a squat one.

"Sounds intriguing." He placed his unlit cigar back in his pocket in favor of the tiny espresso he'd ordered. It smelled delicious and made me want to trade my latte for some "cafecito," as he'd called it.

"I didn't know about the storm when I booked the flight," I said, feeling like an idiot for admitting that. "But it's okay. Coming here has been the most impulsive thing I've ever done. I guess locals don't freak out over the storms like tourists do?"

He shrugged. "Let me tell you something. Key West has seen its share of hurricanes. Storms are nothing to us. Very few ever set us back. This island has seen hundreds of years of horrors and survived it all. We take a lickin' and keep on tickin', you know what I mean?"

"Kind of like the blizzards up North where I come from."

"Somewhat, somewhat. Do you know how Key West got its name?" He possessed the excitement of a teacher who was about to tell me the answer anyway, whether I liked it or not.

I thought of the woman on the plane. "Cayo Hueso something?"

"That's right. It means Island of Bones in Spanish. See, when the Spanish first arrived here in the 16th century, they found the island covered in bones. Piles of them, and nobody around to explain what happened. Creepy, right?"

"Very."

"Nobody is sure if the Calusa had a battle here or if they simply used the island as a mass grave, but I believe they were forced as far south as they could go by another nation before they ran out of land and all perished here in battle."

"Calusa?" I asked.

"Native tribe from Florida. Fishermen, gatherers, peaceful people."

I nodded. I wondered if these Calusa Indians had anything to do with the native man haunting my dreams. I couldn't see how, since I'd started seeing him while I was still in Boston.

Luis continued. "And since Spanish rule eventually led to English rule in the Americas, *hueso* sounded like 'west-o' to the English, so Key West stuck."

"That's fascinating," I said. "I thought it was because Key West was the westernmost key in the US."

"Southernmost. Ninety miles to Cuba." His light blue eyes lost a bit of their sparkle. "There's actually another island just west of here. Dry Tortugas National Park."

"I saw it," I said. "When the sun was going down."

"Yes, exactly."

As fascinating as this was, I needed to take advantage of Luis and ask the questions that didn't have answers on the internet. "Do you know anything about a house called *Casa de los Cayos* out on Roosevelt? It's a small resort inn now. The owner's name is Syndia Duarte. I was told you might. It's now called—"

"La Concha Inn," he finished for me, nodding. "Of course, I do. I would take my guests there every single tour if it weren't so far out of the way. That place is incredibly haunted."

I could've told him that. If I believed in ghosts, that

was.

"How do you know?"

"I've stayed there before. Once. Never heard of it called *Casa de los Cayos,* though." He folded his hands and studied me intently. "Where did you read that? I've read everything there is to know about that place."

"My grandmother lived there," I said. "Long ago. That's what her family called it."

"Fascinating. I did not know that. Did your family speak Spanish?"

"Not that I know of."

"They might have. Many residents here learn it because of our proximity to Cuba. So you're related to the family that lives there now?"

"No, my grandmother came before them. The owners after she left used to be her neighbors. My grandma died last month. I came to spread her ashes, but now it's like I can't leave. There's so much going on, at the inn but also in my head. That's what I wanted to talk to you about."

He lifted his tiny espresso cup and waited for me to clink glasses with him for a toast. "La Concha Inn is one of my favorite topics. And you have me for the next seventy-minutes, Ellie. Ask away."

TEN

"What do you know about the place, about its history? Pretend I'm on your tour and you've taken us out there." I smiled, clasping my hands together.

He slid the dark foamy drink into his mouth, ending with a satisfied grin. "Well, let's see. Captain Robert McCardle owned the place. He used to drive the Havana Ferry back and forth between Key West and Havana. In the early 50s, I believe, he found a bag of gold on his boat and told police about it."

All the same stuff found on the plaque in Syndia's living room at La Concha.

"What else?" I asked.

"But you probably knew all that already," Luis said with side-eye. "You probably want the rest of the story."

"Which is?"

"Which is that Captain McCardle was rumored to have intercepted Captain Bill Drudge's lobster boat at sea after he'd left home on a treasure-hunting expedition."

My grandfather. "Wait, what?"

"I thought that would pique your interest." He bit the corner of his smile.

"Is this common knowledge?"

"Not really, but I've talked to the old folks on this island many years, Ellie. Many years."

"What caused the rumors?"

"The way it happened. Drudge mysteriously went missing days before McCardle came home with a bag of gold when supposedly, he'd been on his shift back from Cuba. How would he have come across that bag on a ferry?" Luis raised an eyebrow.

"That's what I wanted to know."

"Also, records show the Havana Ferry arrived hours late that night. It was supposed to arrive back at 10 PM but finally showed up to port past 1 AM. Drudge's body was never found. Police assumed he became shark food. Soon after, his widow was forced to sell her home—and that became La Concha Inn."

"My grandmother." I stared at him. So strange to hear about my nana from the lips of someone I'd never met who lived so far away from us. "Leanne Drudge."

Luis leaned forward slowly. "Your grandmother was Leanne Drudge?"

"Yes. And Bill Drudge was my grandfather."

His jaw dropped. "You're shitting me."

"I shit not."

"This is amazing. I'm talking to the living granddaughter." He laughed crazily. "Where have you been? Wait, Boston, you told me. And you didn't know any of this until now?"

I shook my head. "My grandmother left Key West soon after her husband died, so I guess she never heard the rumors," I said. "But please, go on."

"Some say your grandmother cursed the place when she left."

I recoiled and narrowed my eyes. "Why would they say that?"

"Well, your grandmother had a reputation for…being different," Luis said, gauging how sensitive I'd be to his choice of words. "Or, for being atheist rather, which, in those times, was practically a sin."

Atheist? She never declared that, but Nana did dabble in natural arts—growing herbs in her garden, astrology, going outside to connect with nature. All when she was younger, while she could still walk. Being outdoors was her religion. I remember her always telling me, *Come look at the full moon, Ellie. It's so beautiful,* when I was little.

But I couldn't see her cursing anyone. "Why would her being atheist make her an outsider?"

Luis shrugged nonchalantly. "Why did they hang women in the Salem Witch Trials? Any woman refusing to take part in a patriarchal religion was considered a witch in those times. In your grandmother's, they couldn't hang anyone, but they could still frown down on them. In fact, the documents from her time were written by churchgoing residents of Key West who believed that a 'wayward woman' lived in that house before the McCardles' daughter moved in."

Her nude pictures. My visions of the witchy neighbor hating her.

"That would explain a lot." I sighed. My grandmother might've been a free spirit who didn't believe in organized religion, but that didn't make her wayward or a witch. I supposed people were scared of anything different in those times.

"You're right. You're absolutely right. Anyway..." Luis leaned back. "About a year or so after your grandfather was declared dead, McCardle died from a heart attack. His son who also worked for the Havana Ferry was laid off when the service closed in 1961, and the old man's wife, Susannah, was said to have gone crazy when she lost her other son to influenza."

"Wow. I didn't know any of this."

"Yep. When the women of the family were unable to

maintain the two homes on their own, they converted the compound to a resort in the seventies to try and make a living."

"There were no other working men to support them?" I asked.

"Her son-in-law cut coquina for a living, the husband of Violet McCardle, but as coquina began running low, he had less and less work. Sometime in the seventies, he was found bleeding to death after getting his arm caught in the circular saw."

Violet McCardle. The old woman who'd died on the dock. Syndia's mother. And could the man I'd seen in the garden have been the other son-in-law? I felt like I was going crazy with bits and pieces of information.

"I don't know what happened to the other sister...there were four siblings altogether," Luis continued, "but one of them ended up staying there and running the motel with her children. After a while, I believe her children left, too. The only one left is Syndia Duarte."

"How do you know so much?" I asked.

"Let's just say La Concha Inn was one of the reasons I moved here. I'd read about it in a few primary documents and the part about a rumored hidden treasure always intrigued me." So, he was another treasure hunter lured to Key West by romance.

"Where are you from?"

"Originally? Havana, Cuba. I came to the US as a child through the Pedro Pan Operation in the sixties. I was raised by family members in Miami, but Key West has always intrigued me. Probably because it's the closest I'll ever get to my homeland again."

No wonder his eyes had darkened upon mentioning Havana. I gave him a sympathetic look. "I'm sorry to hear that."

"It was over fifty years ago now." He sat back and rocked on the back two legs of the chair.

"So, what's with this hidden treasure?" I then asked. "Isn't it just a story to attract customers to the inn? You can't tell me it's actually real."

"Well, that's another one of La Concha's 'legends,'" he said using air quotes. "When McCardle came home, he claimed to have only found a small bag of gold doubloons, but then he bought the house next door, fixed it up really nice, and for a while, the place was show-worthy. One of the nicest homes on the island."

"Why does it look so desolate now?"

"The curse—that's my guess. Seems like the family can't catch a break. Things get worse for them as the generations go by."

"Syndia's mother just died two days ago. I was there."

"Violet?" His eyes widened and he made a *tsk* sound. "I hadn't heard. She was the one to live the longest. I'll have to call Syndia and give her my condolences."

"Why don't you come back with me and tell her yourself? We could use another pair of hands putting up the shutters. She has those old wooden ones. I don't feel very safe." I was beginning to think I should've left the island when I had the chance.

"I don't think she'd be happy to see me. Even though they market the inn as a treasure hunting spot, Syndia has never liked having guests there. It's a slam to their pride. She only displays the treasure memorabilia to sell rooms. She wants to find the gold for herself."

"If it exists," I said.

"If it exists." He smiled. "I know I probably sound like a fool for believing such things, but it's not as far-fetched as you might think. People said that McCardle

81

stole Drudge's treasure then…"

"They killed him right then and there," I finished for him, "fed his body to sharks, which is why they never found him. Is that what happened?"

"We don't know. It's all speculation."

Which is what the tour guide had said at the Hemingway House, that the history of La Concha was speculation and ghost stories at best.

The whole thing sounded like pirates to me. 20th Century pirates. My poor grandfather, finally finding the ship he'd been after only for this man to come along and take it from him then claim to have found it himself. Then, to add insult to injury…he drove my grandmother away and took her house.

"This is all so unfair." I shook my head, staring past Luis into the blurry, rainy window. "I didn't know any of this. My mother doesn't know any of it either."

"Your grandmother did her best to forget it, I would imagine," Luis said.

"Was McCardle a celebrity for saying he'd found gold?"

"For a while, this is why he hid it. To keep people from raiding his home and discovering the rest of the gold. Well, apparently, he hid it too well and it remains hidden to this day. That's how the legend goes."

"Why wouldn't he tell anyone where he'd put it?" I asked, agitated. "What if something bad were to happen to him, which obviously did? Nobody would be able to access it. So, he basically drove his family crazy by not telling anyone the location."

"I have no idea, Ellie. If only I were psychic." He laughed.

I stared at him.

Maybe this was another aspect of the curse, if there

was even such a thing. Maybe part of their misfortune was not being able to enjoy the gold they'd supposedly found. "What about Room 3?" I asked.

He cocked his head suspiciously. "What about it?"

"Why don't they rent it out?"

"It's haunted."

"How would you know?"

"It's the room I stayed in." He raised an eyebrow. "Cold drafts, shutters opening and closing by themselves, the smell of smoke when no one around is smoking..."

"Yes, the same's happened to me, but who's haunting it?"

"That depends on what you experience. If you're asking me, I think they're all there...plus others we don't even know about. Room 3 in particular is a portal of paranormal energy. Even the cat appears there without explanation."

Well, that one I had debunked. Bacon and his secret room. I smiled to myself and cocked my head. "You're eager to believe."

"Ah, the healthy skeptic." Luis smiled. "Look, it's not just me. Countless of guests have said that ghosts haunt La Concha—McCardle, his wife, Susannah, Bill Drudge, the son-in-law...all of them. Maybe your grandmother will join them now that you've spread her ashes."

He'd meant it as funny, and I probably should've been offended, but I wasn't. Part of me wished my grandmother would join them too, so she could kick the ass of every single McCardle asshole who ever ruined her life.

"I'm sorry. I didn't mean it like that." Luis reached across the table to touch my arm. "Sometimes I get caught up in the lore of these haunted locations. I forgot I was talking to someone who actually knew this family.

My apologies."

"It's okay."

These people.

My grandmother.

All my life, Nana had been my mother's mother, my live-in confidant and caretaker, helping my mother raise me when she wasn't able to. She'd cooked, bake, read to me, she'd make key lime marmalade in the kitchen. In later years, she got sicker and less mobile. Ended up in a nursing home. Our job was to keep her spirits up, so she wouldn't think too much of her times here and the life she'd lost. It never occurred to me that she'd have such a complicated history.

My heart ached with a dullness I couldn't put into words. Part of me wished I'd never have opened this can of worms, but now that I had, I had to know it all. Feel it all. Get inside my grandmother's mind. My subconscious knew it, too, hence the visions through Nana's point of view.

"Have you *seen* the ghosts?" I asked.

"I've felt their presence. They appear in photos as orbs of light, ectoplasm, vortices. I'll see if I can find some and send them to you. McCardle is said to haunt the garden and grounds. They sense a negative energy. They feel angry."

"How do we know it's not my grandfather? I would be angry if I were him."

"They see a tall man who fits the description of McCardle. Bill Drudge was shorter and blond, like you, and you're right, he should be angry, but he appears to people as…now this is going to sound crazy, but…"

As he paused, a thought entered my mind. I knew what he was going to say before he said it. My analytical, skeptic mind would never go for an idea like this, and yet

I knew it to be true like I knew my name was Ellie Leanne Whitaker.

"The cat," I said.

"The cat," he agreed, nodding. *How did I know that?* "He's wary of everyone. There are reports of people seeing a man's face, then when they blink, it's the cat. This has been going on for years."

"But Bacon can't possibly be that old."

"Is that the current cat?" he asked. "It's been happening with cats on the property for years. Bacon, the tabby before him, and cats before the tabby... For years and years. According to some, it began with the black cat Leanne left behind."

All I could do was sit there and look at him. So many questions, so overwhelming. "Is that everything you know?"

Luis sighed. "I wish I knew more about La Concha, but Syndia makes things difficult. Not exactly generous with family details."

"Sounds like she's hoarding info or protecting something," I said.

"Or someone. Or a multitude of someones. Generations who've all harbored one big secret—"

"The death of my grandfather," I whispered, staring outside at the light rain spattering the street.

"It's a miracle she even let you in her house."

I turned to watch his eyes carefully.

I had so many questions for Luis, but he didn't have all the answers. I felt unfinished and anxious.

However, the ghosts might know. And if I wanted to hear what they had to say, I'd have to be more open-minded. I'd have to acknowledge that they might exist. Maybe all those times I'd seen them as a child hadn't been OCD. Maybe they'd been real, and the meds had suppressed my ability to sense them.

Luis stretched. "Well, I better get going or my dog's going to wonder if I wandered into a bar after work. Not that it's happened before, mind you." He winked. "Thanks for the talk, Ellie. I'll see if I can go by tomorrow and help Syndia prep the buildings."

"There's something else," I said, reaching into my purse. I pulled out the old key. "I found this in the walls of Room 3. Any idea what it might open?"

His eyes lit up with renewed interest. Treasure-hunting interest. He took the key and flipped it over in his hands. "No, but let's suppose I help you find out...and let's suppose it leads to a finding of the gold doubloon variety...will you share it fifty-fifty?"

From his charming smile, I knew he was joking. Mostly.

"Sixty-forty?" He tried again.

But I didn't care about the gold. I only wanted someone to help me find the things that rightfully belonged to my grandparents, so my nana's soul could rest in peace.

I extended a handshake. "Deal."

ELEVEN

Luis disappeared the same way he'd arrived—by blending into the darkness until I could no longer see him.

I stood on Duval Street and looked around in the lonesome night. Only a few residents remained, hammering wood over their shop windows, while all around, blustery breezes ruffled up the palm trees. It was late, and I hadn't thought about how I would get back at this hour. Even the closest Lyft drivers were an hour away.

According to my map, it would take an hour to get back to the hotel if I walked. I didn't have a choice, so I set about in the direction of Roosevelt Blvd and La Concha Inn. I needed to clear my head anyway.

Nana, why didn't you tell me?

Why did it take death to learn about the people we loved? It was eye-opening to know that a woman I'd loved all my life had been harboring so much pain.

The island was still awake with men working on last-minute shutters and women standing by, handing them panels, drills, or drinks to quench their thirsts. They watched me suspiciously, as though a woman walking alone at night the eve before a storm were a strange sight.

The coffee had woken me up somewhat, and now I felt attuned to everything around me—the swishing palm trees, the oppressive humidity, the singing frogs and crickets, the cats that eyed me from their porches, the distant sounds of boat horns. Residents rocked in their rocking chairs, enjoying the late night winds. The island felt like it sat in the front row of a rollercoaster about to take a plunge. I could almost hear conversations inside of homes, wives asking husbands what would they do if the storm hit harder than expected, ways they could earn income that didn't depend on tourism.

Then there were shadows—dark shadows, dancing shadows, gray in-between shadows, and disappearing shadows. Some shadows seemed to follow me. Some appeared out of dark alleyways only to disappear when I looked at them head-on. Some took the shape of women wearing long dresses with cinched ruffled collars, bustles, and feathered hats until I tried focusing on them.

I rubbed them out of my vision, but after a few minutes, they'd come back.

Soon, the voices began. Muffled, at first. They could've come from second-story open windows or from deep inside the colorful little Victorian homes. But something told me they were around me, following me, begging for my attention.

You are blessed. Speak to me...

"Go away," I told them.

Please...

...if you would only listen...

If I narrowed my eyes, I could almost swear I was a child again, and the voices were bothering me like they did most nights. Men, women, children, people I didn't know, asking me to look at them, to help, to pass on messages. Gripping my head, I almost couldn't take it. I was ready to put on ear buds to drown out the voices.

Then, I paused in my tracks, right there on the

sidewalk. Slowly, I put the ear buds back in my bag. He was there again, my native man standing a few feet away, silently watching. Not menacing, just accompanying me. He was a full-bodied manifestation—of what, I wasn't sure.

My thoughts, most likely.

I could clearly make out his near-naked body, cloth covering his hip section, and a net hanging from his waist. A fisherman. Same face as my dreams, as the glimpses I'd caught of him at La Concha. Clearly, he wasn't tied to any one place.

But he was tied to me. "Who are you?" I asked. "Why do you keep following me?"

He wouldn't answer, and I couldn't stand here all night waiting for a silent Indian to tell me what he wanted. I broke into a fast pace, leaving him behind on the sidewalk, but whenever I'd turn around to check if he was still there, he'd be gone. Then, a minute later, he'd appear ahead of me.

"Tell me what you want," I ordered him, feeling more and more anxious. I didn't like this listening to ghosts thing, but if he had something to say, now was the time to do it before I lost my nerve.

I must've been about halfway to the inn, halfway to insanity, when more figures appeared.

Not all of them from the same time period either. I saw Victorian women, modernly-dressed men and women, and a few children. All of them had been hurt. All of them appeared misty and fog-like bearing touches of crimson. Blood seeping through holes in their chests, to red lines crossing their necks. All of them wanted to tell me how they'd been hurt.

"I can't." I shook my head, releasing the visions, and walking a little faster. *Almost there, almost there...* Each time

I'd close my eyes and open them again, they'd be gone. I couldn't do this. I couldn't be a go-between to these poor souls, though none of them wanted to hurt me.

I thought I could listen, but this was too much. How did mediums handle it? I felt like I was on the edge of a cliff about to fall into a ravine. Reaching into my bag, I took out my pills and swallowed down two more. No water to wash them down. I tried using saliva to do the job, but there they were, dry and blocky in my throat. Did my mother know, believe that I could see them? Did she put me on meds to protect me from the spirits?

Because I could understand that.

I couldn't imagine spending my life having to go through this.

The full-bodied visions went back to being just shadows. The shadows I could handle. As long as they didn't ask anything of me, I could pretend I was on either side of this psychic veil. Right now, I chose to see them as nothing, so I could get home.

Home.

Hilarious.

After a while, I turned down Roosevelt Blvd. with legs burning and chest heaving. Well, what do you know…I'd gotten the ghost walking tour for free. Now I was almost back, and good thing I'd decided to walk the five or so miles from Duval Street, because I needed to crash hard. I needed sleep, rest deeply from overworking my brain all day.

When I finally reached the gate of La Concha Inn, I found it locked. With padlock and everything. "You're kidding me," I said to no one.

Did Syndia not realize I was out or was she deliberately trying to keep me away? I could've easily jumped the fence, but I didn't want to break any rules or act like an interloper. I was a good guest and would behave like one, despite her making things difficult.

Tamping down the inkling of panic in my chest, I pulled out my phone, ready to call the front desk to let her know, when suddenly, the lock twisted and dropped to the ground and the gate opened by itself. A long, loud creak sounded through the stillness. I was almost sure Syndia would hear it and come out.

A gate had just opened by itself.

I swallowed hard.

Something sat in the walkway leading to the house, something small but big for a feline—Bacon. Golden eyes stared at me through darkness, exactly the way a grandfather would if I'd come home too damn late from partying. Tired and full of parental judgment.

"Oh, hey...uh...kitty?" I walked through the gate and brought down the latch over the post. Was Luis right and this cat really embodied Bill Drudge's spirit? It was silly to think, and yet I sort of loved the idea. "Uh, grandpa." I chuckled.

Bacon turned and sashayed back to the front porch, hopping up onto the railing. He was dusty and dirty, and I loved him. Somehow, he belonged to the house, this dilapidated wooden old house with more secrets than Scotland Yard. I reached over to pet him before heading into the house, when for a moment—I saw him.

My stomach leaped into my throat.

Standing behind Bacon in the foliage below, was a handsome man, the kind of wholesome, sunny face that could only belong to a young sea captain. Only he was hurt worse than the others I'd seen on my walk through the island. His red lines were different. His were everywhere—all over his body—like crackled finish on an old painting, though a large one stood across on his neck.

My heart pounded against my ribcage. I got a good look at him. Long enough to see a resemblance with my mother's face and my own. And then I made the mistake of blinking, a habit I'd been doing all night to ward away the spirits. And so he was gone, vanished into the ether.

"Bill." I spoke into the warm night.

Nothing.

Damn it.

Startled, I entered the house, surprised to find the front door unlocked, and ambled down to my room, feeling like I was going crazy. And maybe I was going insane and this was how it felt—like I walked the hedge between the real and imagined. When I unlocked the room and dropped onto the bed, I spotted the window open again and this time, my suitcase looked like it'd been searched through.

"Seriously? Like my undies and shorts, do you, Syndia?"

All the important items were still in my bag—my nana's photos, the key… I thanked myself for thinking to bring it all with me then tucked the stuff under my pillow before falling totally dead asleep. From now on, I'd hang the Do Not Disturb sign, so no one would come in to clean. I hoped the ghosts would read it, too.

The native man was in my room again.

He stood in the corner, gesturing toward the door.

Outside, a storm was brewing. I didn't want to face it, but he insisted, coming to my bed and pulling me to my feet. In my dream, I was naked. Not boudoir naked like my grandmother in her lingerie but completely naked. Vulnerable and exposed. The native man didn't care. He was used to bare skin and I was the fool to think there was anything wrong with it. The wind blew open the shutters again but this time, I didn't bother to fix them.

Come, he said.

What did he want to show me?

His hand was outstretched. I slid my palm into his and felt the dryness of his overworked skin. From his waist, the fishing net hung, no spear. He tapped the mosaic table, as if to tell me there was something meaningful about it.

Then, he led me outside.

Dark storm clouds rolled over the island, and the smell of fish permeated the air. The ground I walked on wasn't soil or even sand. It was crushed shells. Layers and layers of rough crushed shells, much like the kind in the moon sculpture from the garden. There were no quaint Victorian Key West homes, no cars, no tropical charm.

Simply a quiet island covered in crushed shell. We stood on a beach facing the ocean. Down the beach were piles of white sticks growing in size from smallest to largest. Were those bones? Skulls, femurs, tibias, bones and more bones. The man told me what they were in his language, and somehow, I understood him.

They couldn't bury the bones of their fallen victims on this island made of broken shell, so they piled them. They'd died battling other native tribes. I wasn't sure how I knew this, but I bowed my head in respect. Standing still with southern winds grazing over me, I felt at one with the earth. I felt her pain. I felt the plight of these people.

And I felt my own plight as well.

Mayai.

His name was Mayai, and he'd been my grandmother's spirit guide. He'd been my great-great-grandmother's spirit guide before her, and now he was mine. I only needed to listen, though listening was difficult for me. He understood that—I'd been born in a time of tuning out, he said.

But now it was time to let go of barriers.

Mayai used his hands to motion letting go. And I did. With a handful of ashes and bone fragments, I tossed them into the water, into the salty sea, scattering my worries, giving what was once from the earth and ocean back to its origins. With circular, almost spiritual motions, I returned my grandmother to the island she'd loved, the same one that had forsaken her. Now she could rest in peace.

Mayai told me other things without moving his lips. The Spanish ships would not arrive for another several hundred years. Men would obsess over gold though gold belonged to the earth. In the end, nothing belonged to us, except our energy. I wasn't sure what he was talking about, but I would understand it all soon, Mayai told me.

I came from a long line of light workers, women who connected with the universe. Women were better at connecting than men, he told me. I was ready to learn my grandmother's ways, had been since I was a child. But I'd been suppressed, he said. Barriers...time to let go.

In the distance came shouts, words that didn't fit the new language.

I felt myself being pulled away.

"Ellie!"

Mayai nodded with a smile. It was all right. I could go back. I was ready.

"Ellie!"

The sun and ocean quickly darkened into stormy night skies, and I stood on the edge of a dock looking out. No longer naked, I wore shorts and a T-shirt, clothing that brought me back to the present. Was I scattering Nana's ashes again? I looked down at my hands and found my fingers clutching an empty pill bottle. The new Zoloft I'd just bought this morning.

I suddenly remembered where I was, who I was, when I was.

The ashes I'd scattered—they hadn't been. That was a dream.

In real life, they'd been my pills. I'd just tossed my entire bottle of pills into the fucking sea. When I turned around to ask Mayai why he would have me do this, I faced an old woman dressed in black. Wrinkled, vacant staring eyes, her gnarled hands reaching out for my neck. *You killed me. It was you.*

"No, I didn't. Nobody killed you, Violet. You died because you were old." Was I speaking aloud or still in my dream? I wasn't sure. The veil was thin, and I walked the hedge again.

How could you bring that witch's remains back here? I heard her hollow voice as if from another dimension. *How could you bring back the woman who cursed my family's home? Are you hell bent on taking everything from us?*

"My grandmother didn't do anything," I defended. "She didn't do anything. Everything was taken from her!"

The woman's small filmy eyes disappeared into wrinkled skin. The eyeless, faceless visage seemed to implode until she was only a dark mist hovering in front of me.

"Miss Whitaker!" More shouting, as the winds picked up and the rain slammed down on my bare skin in spiky sheets. The old crone disappeared into a vaporous shadow before my eyes, and behind her, standing on the back porch facing the garden was Nottie, waving me inside. "The bands are getting worse. Get inside! It's not safe!"

TWELVE

The longest line I'd ever stood in my life was here and now—at the CVS.

Because of the approaching storm, everybody needed their backup medications in case transportation to and from the island shut down or the pharmacy became damaged. But now that the sun had come out in between feeder bands, we all came out. Waiting forty minutes already under the boiling sun sucked, especially since I'd already refilled these damn pills once before.

Damn Mayai.

He was my spirit guide, he'd said. He'd been my grandmother's before me, and that was fine. I could deal with a hallucination who claimed to be my own protective ghost. What I couldn't deal with was a hallucination claiming to be my protective ghost who made me throw my pills into the ocean. What kind of protection was that?

Because it was time to let go. Time to connect, he'd said.

He didn't understand. He didn't understand what it was like to be an eight-year-old who woke up screaming in the middle of the night, scared to death from all the shadows around her. He hadn't been there, and he wouldn't know the fear, so he shouldn't have made me do that.

Standing in the queue, I seethed. Gritted my teeth.

Others in line had taken to friendly banter, a camaraderie between residents facing peril together, as they talked about the measures they'd taken to protect their homes and the things they still had left to do. The eye of the storm was now passing over eastern Cuba and within hours, conditions would begin to deteriorate.

"Looks good now, doesn't it?" the woman ahead of me said. She knew I was from out of town based on the "friendly banter" she'd tried to have with me, but I'd been too pissed off at the moment to engage. "It always looks this beautiful hours before a hurricane hits. You don't hear birds, do ya?"

"Actually, no."

"Most animals have already taken shelter. Humans are the last idiots outside before a storm, doing final preparations until the last damn moment to pick up their medications." She laughed.

I had to get out of here.

I couldn't stand the sun, I couldn't stand the heat, this woman's friendly face, nothing. And I swore to God, I was going to have an anxiety attack right here in front of everyone. Stepping out of line, I bypassed everyone and charged into the CVS all the way up to the front counter.

"Miss, you have to wait in line," someone said.

I nearly shot them a retort in middle finger form.

Instead, I looked the pharmacist in the eye. "Hi. I already refilled these days ago, but there was an accident, and I honestly can't wait. I need my meds now. Please." I had no idea what I was doing. It wasn't like I'd ever been a diva before. I just knew I felt desperate.

The bespectacled man gave me a thin-lipped grimace. "If it's an emergency, go to the urgent care down the street. They'll take care of you there. I'm sorry...next!" he called, avoiding eye contact with me.

I wanted to knock over the stand holding bags of cough drops, but the last thing I needed was to get arrested for disorderly conduct right before a hurricane. Everyone here was waiting, and everyone had to be patient, including me. But it was hard telling that to my OCD brain.

"Yeah, take your white privilege somewhere else," a man muttered as I charged by.

I stopped to take him in.

Speaking of white, he was bone-colored and wore khaki shorts, a Polo shirt, and nice boat shoes. He'd probably just come from tying up his yacht in the marina. Behind him, a shadow form stood hovering over him. It morphed before my eyes—shifting into a large sunburned man with a noose around his neck. Parts of his hands and body had been charred, and he did not look happy.

"Sir, there's a ghost following you around," I said, focused on the dead man's hollow eyes. "Just a head's up, he'll probably choke you in your sleep tonight."

Then I walked off amid gasps and random insults.

Because screw that guy. And screw Mayai for dumping my pills.

Back outside, my phone rang—my mother's happy face smiling in my hand, but I knew she'd betray that façade the moment I'd answer so I let it go to voicemail. I couldn't handle my mother right now. Whatever she had to say, she'd end up texting it anyway.

Reaching La Concha, I again found the gate locked, but this time, I side-swept it and leaped right over the top. Did I care that my shirt got snagged on one of the pointed tips and I scratched the living crap out of myself? No, because I was quickly reaching my limit of zero fucks given.

I also didn't care when I walked through the front

door and Syndia, talking to Nottie about the potted plants she hadn't brought into safety yet, paused to look at me. "Where do you think you're going?"

"To my room. Room 3, the room where my grandparents used to sleep. Is there a problem?" I pushed past her when she tried getting in my way. I felt like a rebel and I didn't care. This might've been her property now, but in my heart, it was still Nana's and until I helped my grandfather rest in peace, I would never leave.

Terror shone in Nottie's dark eyes. I could only imagine what abuse Syndia had been heaving on her before I walked in. I tried communicating to her without words that she didn't have to stay here, didn't have to take this abuse, but Nottie was stuck as emotional victims tended to be.

"Whitaker, if you won't be leaving, then I'll have to insist that you do something to help us around this place. We are clearly in harm's way while all you do is leave the premises to do God knows what." Syndia's voice grated on my eardrums.

"You mean reordering my medicine?" I strolled up to the plaque over the fireplace and pointed to it. "And finding out from strangers that everything my family loved was taken from them? Yeah, how selfish I'm being." I probably shouldn't have said that, but I was having a harder time than ever controlling myself without my Zoloft.

Bacon darted through the room upon hearing my voice and slammed his body against my legs in jubilation. Syndia, annoyed that her cat favored me over her, cocked her head and took slow steps toward me. "Everything was taken from *you*? *Your* family? You can't be serious."

"I'm dead serious."

"What do you think you know, Whitaker?"

"I know enough." I knew—felt was more like it—that something terrible had happened here and my grandparents had been bamboozled out of money, glory, and a happy marriage they'd both rightly deserved.

"Let me tell you about hard times," Syndia said, picking up her hammer that had been sitting on a table where she'd set it down. My mind without drugs imagined her using that hammer to smash my head into the wall right next to the plaque as a warning to other guests. "You booked five days at a Key West resort for two hundred a night. And that's after paying airfare, rental car, and time off from work. Am I right?"

"You don't know anything about me."

"But I do. I'm guessing you've never had a hard day in your life."

"You don't know that." Emotionally but I had.

"I know plenty," she said. "I know you brought Leanne Drudge's ashes here to spread all over my house. I know that you see ghosts."

What? How would she know that?

She giggled at the confusion on my face. "You think you're the only one to see them? They talk to me, too. Why do you think this place is called one of the most haunted spots in Key West? And not in the good, touristy way," she said. "In the nobody-wants-to-stay here way."

"If they talk to you, too, why won't your grandfather tell you where the treasure is?" I asked. "Problem solved." She was bluffing, just like she was bluffing about knowing I could see spirits. "None of this has to do with what happened here in 1951, Ms. Duarte."

"But it does. Your family had enough money to have your grandmother cremated whereas I had to leave my mother with the coroner down at the county. Do you know how much her Medicaid covered?" Syndia slowly encroached in my space.

"I'm sorry about your mother, Ms. Duarte."

"Fifteen hundred, Whitaker." She took slow steps towards me. I backed up, not liking the way she was approaching. "Fifteen hundred, and you know how much a basic funeral costs? You would know. Seven thousand five-hundred. So you see, you ended up better off than I did in the long run. So, why are you here? Can't you leave us alone?"

I felt bad that she and her family had had a hard time all these years, but their choices had been her own. They could've sold this place a long time ago and moved somewhere cheaper, just like Nana had to do.

"You think this is about money?" I spat, backing away. "You keep thinking that. I don't want anything belonging to you, Syndia. All I want is to find out the truth. My family has a right to know what happened here."

"Your family lost its rights, information included, the moment your grandmother sold the house. You shouldn't have stepped foot in here."

, "It was my grandmother's wishes to be here," I said. "Your life is based on a lie, Ms. Duarte. The least you can do is allow me to find the truth."

She scoffed and turned away, sending Nottie into the backyard to finish bringing in the plants.

"This place of yours is built on lies," I told her, entering the outside corridor. "The truth will always come out, and that's been happening since the day my grandmother died." Even more so since I spread her ashes. Maybe Nana's presence agitated the haunting, got all the spirits out of sorts, her return to *Casa de los Cayos* awakening every resting soul on this property.

"How do you know that?" Her voice shook, and that

glass eye of hers stared right through me with its lifeless sheen. "How do you know the truth always comes out? Google tell you that?"

"No, your house does. It speaks to me at every turn, tells me more and more each day." I backed off, keeping an eye on Syndia as I felt my way backwards down the hall.

Chewing her bottom lip as she used the hammer to pound a plank of wood against a room door, I knew that Syndia was losing her shit. This woman was crazy. Like I'd lost it at CVS earlier but at a much more psychotic level, because she had more to lose than I did. Even I went home now, I'd be no worse off than when I'd left.

I had to watch myself around her. She stood to lose her home if she couldn't pay it, she'd lost her mother to strangers who would burn her flesh then never return an ounce of her ashes, and now, a storm was on its way, threatening everything she had.

The more I gained, the more she lost.

And that made me her enemy.

THIRTEEN

I was more nervous about Syndia than the coming storm. Which, according to the latest advisory, would be starting very soon, with the eye wall passing over Havana, Cuba by tomorrow evening, putting us in the northwest sector.

I did my best to help her by bringing in loose items from the yard, anything that could become a projectile—empty pots, old yard toys, loose pieces of wood, which I piled inside the living room to use for shutters. La Concha didn't have any of the fancy metallic hurricane shutters I'd seen down on Duval Street that closed shut like an accordion.

No, here, we had to hold the pieces up and drill them into the wooden structure of the house. It was easy to see where former shutters had once been drilled. The holes were still there, and we couldn't use them or the screws would come right out. Hence, Syndia had to drill in new places, which only made the house look worse.

After a couple of hours, she grew tired. The woman might've been over fifty, but she was a beast for having such a small frame. Around five, I sat inside the living room to watch the latest advisory and while Syndia disappeared to another part of the house, saw that tornadoes had been spotted all along the lower keys.

Great. Tornadoes. *Yay.*

I checked my phone and saw at least a hundred texts from my mother and friends back home. I gave everyone the same copy-and-pasted quick reply letting them know I was fine. And then, someone called from a 305 number. Though I hadn't programmed it into my phone, I had a feeling who it was and answered on the second ring.

"Hello?"

"Ellie from Boston!" Luis's cheery voice rang through the line. It was nice to hear a voice I recognized that wouldn't judge me for staying in town instead of fleeing the storm like it was out to kill me.

"Hey, Luis. How's it going?"

"Just finished up helping my landlord with the sandbags, thought I'd check in on you to see if you and Duarte needed anything."

Nottie eyed me curiously from the front office. I sank into the corner to talk privately. "Actually, it's just me and her putting up shutters. The older woman's doing what she can. I honestly don't know if they're going to hold. We're running out of steam here."

"I told you I'd come by to help if you needed it."

"I think we need it."

"I'll be there in thirty minutes. Syndia won't like it, but try to convince her it's for the best. See you soon."

"Will do." I hung up and grabbed a plastic cup of water from a pitcher Nottie had put out for us.

"What is it that we need?" Syndia asked me, coming back in.

"Oh, help with the shutters," I told her. "A friend of mine in town said he would help when he was done with his, so I told him to come over. Hope that's okay."

"It's not okay. I don't have anywhere to put him up during the storm. All the rooms are filled with outdoor furniture and things."

It wasn't true. There wasn't much outside but the broken lounge chairs and a mess of wild foliage. "I don't think he plans on staying," I explained. "He only wants to help. I mean, you want to be absolutely sure that our shutters are secure, don't you? Make sure the house sustains minimal damage? It's good to have a man around for the hard stuff."

It was an awkward, sexist thing to say, but I knew it would appeal to her older woman sensibilities, and it worked. She shrugged, going back inside the office. "But he can't stay."

"No worries there. But I will ask him to," I muttered under my breath. "If I feel unsafe around you."

Before Luis arrived, I texted him to come around the side of the property where he could wedge his way in unseen through the guest gate. I didn't want Syndia turning him away before he had the chance to help.

I was near the spot where I'd seen that bloody ghost, and my nerves were on high alert waiting for a similar experience—the cold shiver up my arms, the frozen spot inside my torso, my inability to move. The rain had started again but it felt good to be outside, absorbing its energy. Somehow, it recharged me, made me feel I could handle anything.

I stood by the back wall of the last guest room, chewing on my nails. If I closed my eyes, I could feel them staring. The shadows. The spirits. Wanting to come near me, wanting to tell me things. *No, no, no...* I shook my head and tried to stay on this side of the veil.

According to Mayai, it was time to let them in. Time to listen and connect, but I just couldn't do it. I kept my eyes wide open, focusing on the smallest of things—the raindrops falling off the eaves, the lines and patterns in the hibiscus bush leaves next to me. Anything but staring into space. That was when they started to come out.

I was scanning the yard, waiting for a sign from Luis, when I spotted something in the corner of the yard. Covered in vegetation, it could've been anything, but the dull gray metal and patches of reddish stain told me it was discarded machinery. Slowly, I stepped through the leaves over to it, only to find it was larger than I originally thought, about six feet wide and four feet tall, a massive thing with gears and dull blades and curved parts to protect the user.

It must've been half a century old.

It was covered in rust and I felt stupid for not being able to identify it. All around me, mosquitoes flitted and landed on my skin, looking to feast. I knew I had to move out of this corner quickly, else become their latest meal. But I couldn't move. I was drawn to this machine and its once-sleek design.

It might've been a strange lawnmower or an old air conditioner unit out here rotting in the wild, but whatever it was, it had taken a hold on me. Lightly, I ran my fingertips along its frame, stopping to close my eyes and just feel.

Them blades will get duller, if you do, then you won't be able to use it no more.

If they do, I'll just sharpen them up again.

Two men talking around me, two men from long ago. One was the operator of the machine. The other was his father-in-law. Hunched over the first man, he watched with great scrutiny, making sure he did everything right. A lot was riding on his ability to perform this task.

On the grass between them was a third man.

Unmoving, lying on the ground. Wasn't a part of the conversation at all. In fact…

I ripped my hand away from the metal. "What the hell?"

"Ellie."

I whirled around. Luis stood there in shorts and T-shirt, looking way more casual than I'd seen him the other night. My head spun with heavy unseen energy. "You scared me."

"I'm so sorry. You told me to come this way, so I did."

"Yes...thank you. I just..."

He put a hand on my shoulder. "Are you okay? You look like you're about to faint. It's damn hot out here, that's for sure."

"Yeah, I didn't expect this much heat. But um..." Ask Luis, my intuition told me. If anyone would know, it'd be him, and something told me he already knew what was wrong.

"Oh, wow, is that what I think it is?" He navigated through the dense undergrowth, stepping over rough-cut stones I hadn't even realized were there. "I've never actually seen one of these before."

"What is it?"

"For cutting stone. Remember I said McCardle's son-in-law cut coquina for a living? This must've been his tool for doing just that. See these rocks all around?" He pointed to the porous gray stones that looked like they'd been eaten by acid. "That's coquina."

"They're everywhere in this yard," I said.

"Yes, the seawall is made out of it too. It stretches all the way down. About an acre wide. Anyway, just tell me where to start." He surveyed the buildings from where we stood. "I see these rooms over here still need shutters. Got any wood?"

I pointed to the pile we'd collected from scattered

junk piles, and as Luis headed off in that direction to fetch the planks, the visions returned. I felt the heat stir around me, the ground tilt on an axis, and suddenly, I was there again, watching the two men discussing the machine and its blades.

The third man lay still on the ground. I knew he was dead but didn't want to look at him directly. Whether or not this was my imagination or real, it felt real. Who was he? And what were they about to do? I got a sinking feeling in the pit of my stomach so hard, I had to turn away and suddenly, I heaved the contents of my stomach into the grass.

Bacon came by at just that moment and meowed, sniffing around my feet.

I kicked him aside so he wouldn't mess with the vomit. "Go on, get out of here." I shooed him. He did, only in the direction I didn't want him to—toward the machine. He leaped up onto it, did a circular walk, then growled in the direction of the men I'd seen. Men who were there. Not visions in my mind, but actually there. They'd lived here long ago. Hissing at empty air, Bacon jumped off the machine and ran through the yard.

The last thing I saw was the dead man's leg being twisted like a chicken drumstick by one of the other men. I wasn't sure which because I could barely keep it together. But Mayai would've wanted me to stay calm, open up, listen and connect, so I tried. I tried so hard, but it was taking every ounce of energy out of me. They were tearing this man apart, for crissake.

Then, I saw it—the hatchet coming down, slicing right underneath the knee cap, taking the man's leg right off, pant leg and all. *Skin him good,* the man said. *The less meat, the better.*

I couldn't take it anymore and turned to run, but as I

did, I smacked right into a human wall. I screamed, and even as I heard Luis's voice telling me it was okay, to calm down, I still couldn't shake the terror of what I'd seen out in the yard. He put down two planks of wood to hold my shoulders. "Hey, hey, it's me."

I slammed my fists against his chest, pushing away what I thought was the image still in front of me. What had that been? Why was I seeing this?

"What did you say that was used for again?" I pointed to the machine I couldn't look at anymore. The rusted machine out in the corner of the property.

"For cutting coquina," he said, helping me stand straight again. "The shell rock forms naturally over thousands of years, but it's incredibly hard. They used to use all sorts of tools for shaping it. I don't think it's harvested anymore. Real coquina is hard to find these days. A lot of what you see is fake. Are you okay? Did something spook you?"

I couldn't answer. I had to know more. "What else is it used for?"

"That's it, as far as I know. Well..." He raised an eyebrow.

I didn't like the look in his eye. Yes, Luis was an entertainer of sorts, as tour guides tended to be, and he loved the drama of a good story, but I knew what he was going to say next because of the vision I'd seen. And my body chilled up, paralyzing me to my core.

"Some say that human bones are ground up and used to make *manmade* coquina. All mixed up with the shell and limestone. Nobody would ever know because it all looks the same, but that's just stuff we guides tell people on ghost tours to scare them. I've never actually heard of or seen evidence of it."

I had.

Human bones. De-fleshed and ground up. I'd seen it played out live right in front of me. But I couldn't speak, couldn't tell him what I'd seen. I only closed my eyes one more time and, despite me trying to keep it together, the world went black around me.

FOURTEEN

Mayai was back. We were on a new part of the island.

He showed me the ships, the Spanish ships, that had wrecked on the shore, and the inhabitants, including Mayai, salvaging wood, working together to put them into piles. A new industry for the Calusa emerged—wrecking. This was one of the last times the Calusa would live on this land. Soon, more ships would come, and the tribes would scatter. Many would be killed. Some would flee on boat to Cuba.

It was hard to know who to trust, Mayai said.

Sometimes the Spanish were friendly. Other times, they arrived deranged and ready for war. If it wasn't the Spanish killing the English, it was the English killing the Spanish, and the innocent ones aboard looked to the native people for sanctuary. Many of them lived amongst them for years. Many bred and began families.

I came from one of those mixed families.

I had part European and part indigenous Floridian in me.

Mayai was one of my ancestors.

The blackness in my peripheral melted, as my eyes adjusted to my surroundings. I was in a room, not on a beach with Mayai, and I quickly recognized the space. Room 3. A man was by my side, peering into my face as he hovered over me. "Ellie, you okay? You blacked out. What happened out there?"

"Huh?" I sat up and blinked, head pounding. It took me a moment then I remembered. "I saw something."

"A ghost?" Luis asked hopefully, childlike wonder in his eyes.

"More like a scene, a reenactment of something that happened long ago."

"A residual haunting." He rubbed his chin. "What did you see?"

I wasn't sure I wanted to tell him. But I felt so alone just then, a world away from my life in Boston with one foot in this new world in Key West that I needed to. Connection. Someone who would understand. "I saw two men operating that machine. And...it wasn't pretty."

"Tell me," Luis said. I got the sense he was more interested to hear my ghostly tale than he was about getting me to feel better. "I mean, if you feel comfortable."

"I don't."

Suddenly, a female silhouette blocked the open doorway. "Who are you? Why are you here?" It was Syndia, filling the frame despite her thinness.

I tried to stand to explain, but lost my balance and sat on the edge of the bed again. My grandmother used to sit on the edge of this bed, too. I wasn't sure how I knew that but the information coming at me lately felt real and trustworthy. "This is my friend who lives in Key West. The one I told you about," I explained. "He came to help us put up shutters."

"Luis Gallardo," she said with a wary, deep tone. "We don't need any more help."

"Hello again, Ms. Duarte. Nice to see you," Luis said, offering his handshake. "She fainted outside, and I think having another hand to help would be beneficial to you."

"I don't care what you think," Syndia snapped, rejecting his handshake. I wondered what Luis had done to make him unwelcome here. If he was anything like me, it didn't take much. "You asked too many questions last time."

"I won't ask any this time," Luis promised. "Trust me."

"The winds are due to arrive by tonight," I said. "We've only covered half the windows. I think you should let him help us."

She glared at us a second more, sizing Luis up. Then, she turned around and left the room. A moment later, I heard the sounds of wood being dragged down the hallway and being plopped down. Banging of planks.

Luis turned back to me. "Told you she doesn't like me."

"She doesn't like anybody," I said. "What did you do?"

"I asked her mother's nurse questions about the family, the ghosts, the gold, because she seemed amenable to answering, and Duarte nearly bit my head off."

"Same thing happened to me. It was like Nottie had said too much."

"Yes, exactly."

"But right now, Duarte doesn't have much of a choice," I said. "I don't see neighbors clamoring to help this woman put up shutters." I rubbed my eyes and worked on focusing my attention, not an easy task without my meds.

We had to finish preparing the house.

I had to pretend I hadn't just seen a dead man's leg get chopped off for what I could only assume was to be fed into a grinding machine. A machine used to pummel shell, not human bones. What horrors had happened in this area since my grandmother left? Who would do such a thing?

"You were telling me about your vision?" Luis asked.

I decided I would tell Luis my story after he'd helped us. Once he'd assisted us with boarding up, I'd reward him. "We'll have plenty of time for chatting later," I said. "Let's get the last of the windows covered up before the next rain band comes through."

Getting up to stretch, my gaze landed on my purse sitting on the mosaic table. It was open and looked as though rifled through. "What the…" I flew over to it and checked inside. The photos were there, but I couldn't find the brass key anywhere. "Where's the key?"

"The what?"

"The key! The key!" I stammered, taking everything out of the purse and flipping it inside out. "Did you take it?" I zeroed in on Luis.

"No. You've seen my whereabouts the whole time I've been here, Ellie. Besides, I don't steal." He was indignant, and it occurred to me how I knew absolutely nothing about the man in my room. He could've been a thief or a murderer, and I'd just invited him here assuming he'd be safe.

No, he's fine and he's safe, I reminded my OCD. The world would not fall apart around me. "I was out for a while, wasn't I?"

"Yes, you fainted, but I didn't take your key."

Then who did? For all I knew, that key didn't lead to anything significant, and here I was panicking for no reason. But something told me that it did, and my intuition, if anything, had been getting nothing but stronger since I'd arrived.

Luis threw up his hands and walked out of the room. "Esta mujer, coño," he said to zero understanding on my part. "You know what? I didn't come here to get accused of stealing, so I'll be heading back now. Good luck with the storm."

"No, wait." I began rushing out then turned back around, placed my purse inside the hole in the wall behind the safe, then stepped into the corridor. "Luis, I'm sorry. I'm not feeling well. I shouldn't have accused you."

"Listen, I'm only here to help you out."

"You're also here in hopes of finding treasure." I lifted an eyebrow. I mean, it was true. "Let's not kid ourselves. You said so yourself. You can see how I might've mistrusted you for a second there."

"Yes, but we had an agreement. We said if I help you find that gold, we'd share it. I wouldn't try and find it myself, I wouldn't take your key without asking, and I sure as shit wouldn't worry about it now when a storm's on the way."

"Fine, I'm sorry. And shh. Don't talk about the gold out loud. You-know-who is somewhere nearby, probably eavesdropping." I craned my neck looking for Syndia, heard banging, hammering noises at the opposite end of the property.

"Fine." Luis pulled planks of wood off the ground and began dragging them toward the guest room without boards up on their windows.

I sighed and rubbed the stress from my face, glancing in the direction of the machine again. Nothing there but shrubbery. But something lingered, something watched from the trees. I hated the feeling that sank deep into my skin.

Following Luis, I again told myself to stay focused, worry about the storm right now. That was top priority, and we'd figure the rest out at a later time. We only had a few hours left to prepare.

The gusts of wind were getting stronger. Palm fronds blew intermittently like long green and brown hair being blow-dried by an unseen force. The giant banyan tree in the center courtyard swished in the wind. I felt chilled even though it was hot outside. Walking through the garden, I again got that heavy feeling like someone was watching, like this center hub was also the heartbeat of the property.

I stopped to close my eyes, sensing my surroundings better this way.

Behind the banyan tree, someone stood near the moon sculpture. Watching me, though there was no one. No one corporeal anyway. I heard Maya's voice near my ear—*they took our land once before. Fight. Don't let them take it again.*

He meant my dream while I'd been passed out. I now remembered it—the ships, the bloodshed, his telling me that I was descended from his tribe mixed with Europeans. "I *am* fighting," I murmured, continuing to walk around the circular stone wall. "I'm here, aren't I?"

I'd stayed on the island fully knowing that a hurricane was on its way, fully knowing that it was crazy to do so, to stay with a woman who was unstable at best.

I stared at the moon sculpture so hard, I felt it would fall over and shatter. Suddenly, Bacon appeared, leaping out through the bushes, positioning himself between me and whatever unseen presence was in the garden. He hissed, baring his sharp teeth and flattening his dirt-filled ears.

Summer gnats flew around his face and occasionally flitted around mine as well.

"What's wrong?" *Bacon, Grandfather, whoever you are…*

Luis called for me, but I was rotted to my spot. Fear and paralysis seized me. I could only stare ahead. I was sure if I waited long enough, something, or someone, would materialize. And as much as I didn't need more distraction, I couldn't look away.

I was about to wrench myself away when the winds kicked up another notch. The blustery breezes whipped the palm fronds high above. *Go away, Ellie,* another voice spoke to me. My grandmother. *Go away, now.*

"Nana? Where are you?"

Go away. Your job here is done.

"No, it's not. They took your house, your husband, your fortune..." I spoke to the emptiness in front of me. My job had been to spread her ashes, but my goals had changed. I wanted to put an end to this messed-up family's reign. I wanted to give my grandmother back everything she'd lost.

If Mayai was right, and we were descendants of this land, then that pissed me off even more. We'd ended up in Boston, for crying out loud, instead of living out our days here in Cayo Hueso at *Casa de los Cayos,* my family home.

My soul filled with anger when I thought about all that might have happened over the years. I took the offenses personally as if they'd happened to me. In a way, they had. My hands balled into fists, and I wanted to scream. Inexplicably. Furiously. I knew it'd cause alarm and Syndia, Nottie, and Luis would come running, so I held it in as long as I could.

They'd taken it all away. Foul play.

I had no evidence. None—zero.

Except for these voices and visions.

Like the one that spiraled into my view this very second. As Bacon continued to hiss, the gnats that had been bothering him before formed a large cloud of even more tiny insects until they took the shape of a man. A tall man made out of swirling bugs with a face, fierce grimace, and everything. Handsome, formidable. Cruel smile. He held a long blade smattered with dark red. The entire vision was comprised of the flying insects.

I couldn't move, couldn't scream, just like my night terrors when I was a child. Powerless to do anything. But I could speak and forced myself to utter a few words.

"McCardle…" The winds shot through the garden as though controlled by the apparition himself. Behind him, the massive banyan tree swayed. Loose, dried palm fronds fell to the ground, one of them nearly hitting Bacon.

Get out of here, the specter hissed at me.

"I will not," I said, feeling my grandmother's hand slipping into mine and drawing me away. But that had to be a desire of my damaged brain, because she wasn't here. None of them were here, and Bacon was merely hissing at the wind. The battle waging was all in my head.

"Ellie!" Luis called from somewhere.

I couldn't reply, though I understood his concern. A force was coming from the inlet, something headed this way. I felt the salty spray of ocean mist cover my face. Whatever it was, it was rogue and wild and spontaneous, appearing randomly out of nowhere.

"Ellie!" I heard Luis's call even closer.

Ahead of me, McCardle's ghost yelled, louder than before—*GET OUT OF HERE!* His voice boomed throughout the garden, just as a pair of warm, humanly arms wrapped around my torso and pulled me backwards. A half a second later, a vortex of spinning water engulfed one of the palm trees and ripped it right out of the ground, sending it shooting through the air and crashing toward us. Its thorns tore long stinging lines through my leg.

Shit.

Luis tumbled to the ground with me in his arms, and we landed underneath the overhang by the atrium. Overhead, the spinning watery tornado cut a course over the house, ripping off a few shingles then it was gone.

"Holy shit…" Luis gasped for air.

"What was that?" I cried.

"Water spout," he said, chest heaving. "The moment I saw those palms kick up and tasted the salt in the air, I knew what was coming."

I forced myself to move, to shake off the shock.

I couldn't imagine how bad the actual hurricane would be if that had only been a precursory waterspout. What had I gotten myself into? But had the spout come naturally or had McCardle caused it? I couldn't believe I was even asking myself such a question.

"Thank you." I sat up and hugged Luis. No, I didn't know him more than a hole in the wall, but he didn't have to save me. He could've let me die then fended for himself. But he didn't. And right now, that made him my only friend on this island.

You should've let her die.

The words were not of this world, and I was getting tired of these ghosts messing with me, their hateful messages echoes of an era left behind. They were ethereal and evil and full of spite, and it was no wonder my grandmother left this town. When I looked up at the cloud of gnats again, I saw the final wisp of McCardle glaring down at us, his wife Susannah by his side.

FIFTEEN

"I'm sorry. I have to go lie down." I rushed out of there as quickly as I could and headed to my room. I felt Luis following me and hesitant to come in, so he hovered by the open door.

"What happened out there?" he asked. "Something's going on."

"No shit something's going on," I snapped back then pinched the bridge of my nose. "I can't explain it."

"You were in some kind of a trance. I kept calling you."

"I know, I could hear you, but I couldn't move. I saw him."

"Saw who?"

"McCardle. I know it was him. I've never seen him, but I just knew somehow. He caused that water spout."

Luis narrowed his eyes a bit. "Ellie, I believe that you saw him. I told you many people do, but that spout...that's a normal occurrence in these weather conditions. He couldn't have—"

"I'm telling you, he caused it!" I snapped again. "You're the one person I know who believes in strange occurrences, and even you're telling me you don't believe in a strange occurrences. Jesus Christ!"

"Alright, look. I believe you, okay? I'll believe anything that happens here. Like I told you the other night, I would bring my tour groups here if Syndia allowed it. Also, if it weren't so…"

"Cursed?"

"I guess that would be the word, yes."

Bacon appeared behind Luis but didn't rub against his legs. He merely looked up as if waiting for an invitation. "Is this Bill Drudge reincarnated?" Luis asked with a laugh.

"I've no clue. Psst, come here, Bacon…" I whistled and snapped my fingers to get him to come in, but he refused. When I got up to pet him, Bacon walked a little further away. When I was nearly close enough to scratch his head, he moved a little further away again.

"I think he wants me to follow him," I said, remembering his hiding spot and my grandmother's photos. "He's led me to objects before."

"Fascinating." Luis crossed his legs and watched as Bacon led me back down the hallway, stopping midpoint to make sure I was still behind him then leading me into the other half of the property. The McCardle-Duarte side of the property on which I'd never been.

"I can't go that way," I told the cat.

"You have to." Luis raised an eyebrow.

"Well, then you're going to have to distract Syndia. Take her to Home Depot or something. Tell her you're out of screws. Anything."

"I'm on it. I'll text you when we're gone." Luis pulled out his keys from his pocket and spotted Syndia coming out of the front office. "Ms. Duarte?" He blocked my line of view, giving me a moment to hide inside an alcove. "Could you come with me to get some materials while Ellie is lying down?" He disappeared into the main house. "She's still not feeling well, and I could use the extra hands…"

Down the corridor, Bacon meowed impatiently.

"I'm coming," I whispered. Nervously, I glanced everywhere and practiced an excuse in my head in the event that Syndia came back in and found me trespassing in her home. "I was just looking for Nottie," I muttered out a fake reason. "Hoping she could give me some aspirin."

Yeah, right.

I prayed to the universe that nobody would catch me in here. The thought that Syndia might have video cameras throughout the house suddenly occurred to me, but then I remembered that Syndia couldn't even afford a new coat of paint, much less high tech.

I followed Bacon to the last room on the left, entered the house, and was not too surprised to find it utterly cluttered. Newspapers, magazines, and boxes covered any view of the walls. More boxes filled with old electronics, wires, and busted light bulbs. Cassette tapes and old headphones, but I couldn't stop to take stock of any of these things. I had to follow the cat.

"Where are you taking me?" I stepped up to a flight of stairs and got a buzz in my pocket. The text from Luis. I glanced at it to make sure I was clear to go upstairs.

She didn't want to go but I said it was imperative. So we're out. Hurry.

Got it, I replied then headed up the stairs.

Bacon meowed again then turned the corner while I thought about all the ways my life had changed in just the four days I'd been here. Here I was, following a cat through a house not my own, out of sheer certainty that he was leading me to something important.

Once upstairs, I caught sight of a gray dusty tail entering a room on the right. Following the tail, I entered what appeared to be a guest bedroom overtaken by more stuff. Boxes and old furniture sat over rust-colored shag carpet. This had to be a breeding ground for fleas. Bacon bumped his side against an old cardboard box.

"You want me to open that?"

Bacon meowed in response.

Quickly, I pulled the lid of the box and found old photos tossed inside. No rhyme or reason. Just a box of random photos, many black-and-white but most of them faded 1970s specials. "I can't take that, Bacon. And going through it would take forever." Still, I kneeled and rifled through the box, jumping at every sound I heard. "Damn it, my nerves."

There were family photos of what I assumed were the McCardles' children and grandchildren in their younger days living in Key West. One after the other. The further I dug, the older the photos got. I had no idea what this cat wanted me to find, and now that I thought about it, I felt even more stupid for believing such a thing.

"You just want attention, don't you?" With my nerves in my throat at the thought that someone could come in any minute, I thought about abandoning this lovely trespassing adventure and returning to my room.

But then I pulled out one particular black-and-white photo—the mosaic table inside Room 3, only it wasn't. It just looked like it but on a grander scale. On the wall was a large, mural-type mosaic covering at least a quarter of the little room. It was hard to tell what the image was, since the photo was mostly gray and had faded even more since it had been taken, but it seemed to be a map of the Lower Keys and Cuba.

I heard a shuffling outside the window. I parted the sticky old blinds and saw Nottie quietly sweeping the grounds. I let out a breath of relief. Did she not know that this place was about to get messy as hell? Sweeping would not help La Concha look any better, and after the storm, it would be even worse. She had to be doing something to get her mind off other things.

Cold air filtered into the room. There was no A/C on. This made the hair on my arms stand straight up. I knew it wasn't coming from anywhere in particular. "Who's there?" I'd almost completely accepted that the ghosts ruled this resort, and I was no one to question their existence.

I heard a car door slam.

Shit. I had to get out of here.

I hadn't found anything spectacular but these photos were interesting. Plucking out as many of the series I could find, I closed the box and hugged them close. A few days ago, I wouldn't have worried about Syndia but now I hated to think of what she'd do if she found me in here.

Hurrying back the way I came, I paused downstairs just outside the door, sweat pouring down the sides of my face. Bacon ran out before me while I hung back in that smoky, nasty room waiting for the right moment to leave. I listened. When I saw Syndia enter the yard, heard Luis's voice, and noticed that I'd missed a text (*on our way back*) my heart shot into my throat.

Shit, shit, shit…

How could I escape this room without Syndia seeing me?

Not only that, but Nottie was still near the door sweeping the sidewalk, talking to herself. In her own little world. From the way she appeared to be lost in thought, you'd have never known that hurricane winds would be starting soon. I could dart out and make a run for it, but that might cause alarm. I could also quietly wander out and pretend like this was all normal. I opted for the latter.

But then, I felt the chill return. Someone was following me—someone in the spirit world. The chill turned into shadows in the corner of my eye, and I knew then that I wasn't alone. I didn't want to see them, though. Didn't want to face them again. Enough ghosts for one day.

Bacon rubbed up against Nottie's legs and meowed loudly.

"What you want, cat? I fed you three times. Fine, let's go eat again." She rested the broom against the wall, and I sank back into the shadows until she'd passed. Nottie was gone for the moment, but now I had to get past Syndia out in the yard looking for more items to bring inside.

As I nonchalantly scuttled down the corridor, Luis caught sight of me and gave me a questioning look, like why was I still on the wrong side of the property. He began to talk to Syndia again loudly, so as to cover up any noise I might make behind her, and I knew that was my cue to get my butt moving.

"What do you have on that side of the yard over there?" he asked her, shooing me away behind her back.

"You said you wouldn't ask questions," Syndia replied flatly.

"I was talking about your famous legend. And your ghosts. This is about your yard."

She sighed, annoyed at Luis's presence. "A few tires. The old shed we don't use anymore. Just another thing to fix." She scoffed. "Let's get these last boards up, so I can rest and you can leave."

"Yes, ma'am," Luis said. "I just need to use the restroom. Would you excuse me a moment?"

I shuffled all the way into Room 3 and closed the door knowing that Luis would be right behind me any moment. He cracked the door open and stepped inside.

"Where were you? Didn't you get my text?"

"I didn't notice. I was busy looking at photos."

"Of what?"

"Of this." I handed him the old black-and-whites and stood there, hand on chin, wondering where this mosaic would be today. "Have you seen it here before?"

"Not that I can recall."

"Is it hard to take down a mosaic, you think?" I asked.

"You mean by tearing down little piece of tile by little piece of tile? I would think so, yes. Probably easier just to cover it up. Why?"

I was staring at the wall opposite the bed. It was old and stained and cracked, but that was a beautiful thing. It'd be easier to break apart. "Have any screws in your pocket?" I asked. Glancing at the mosaic table, I went up to it and crouched to the ground, looking up at the underside. A handwritten inscription was there in faded ink: *For my love...1949.*

My grandfather. Another handmade gift to my grandmother.

He reached into his pocket and produced a long wall screw for securing boards. "Am I a handy man, or what?" He laughed. "I have to get back outside before she comes looking for me. We got to Home Depot and when she saw the line for wood, she made me turn around. Didn't want to leave you alone, I guess."

"Yeah, untrustworthy me. It's okay. It gave me enough time." I held up the photo and compared it to the wall. Then, I walked up to the crack in the left third and used the screw to chip away the plaster.

"What are you...oh...you think that mosaic is still under there?"

I didn't just know it. I could see it in my mind. It was

colorful and matched the small table etched with my grandfather's initials. In fact, I'd seen it several times as a child. It hadn't been just a dream. It had existed for real. And it was behind this wall.

SIXTEEN

Repetitively, I scratched at the wall with the screw.

It may not have been the best of tools, but it was enough to loosen the chipped sections of the exposed crack. "I bet you anything…"

Bet that this mosaic was underneath this plaster. If my grandfather had made this table, then he definitely made the wall mosaic, too, and where else would it be but in this room? The room Bacon preferred. The room I'd envisioned myself in as Nana. This had to have been their room—my grandparents'. The McCardles and Duartes had tried to cover over it, remove all traces of the family who'd once inhabited here.

My family.

"They used plaster instead of drywall," Luis said, grabbing another screw and helping me chip away. "Why wouldn't they just cover it up in one piece? So much easier."

"Exactly. One piece comes off too easily," I said. My fingertips were beginning to get sore from the awkward scratching of wall with a rusty screw. "If they smeared over the mosaic with plaster, it's because they didn't want anyone to ever see it again. They wanted to cover it nice and good."

This house dripped with oddities. Between the cold drafts, the visions, the mysterious holes in walls, disappearing keys, and a resident cat who knew the place like a former owner would, I quickly learned not to be shocked by anything anymore. Still, I had to find that key. If Syndia stole it back, it had to be important.

Our chipping at the wall created two little piles of white dust on the floor that danced in the vortices of the rogue wind entering the room. We scraped away in silence for ten minutes without revealing anything. Finally, it occurred to me what was wrong—we were working on the wrong wall.

"Stop," I said, catching my breath. "See the way the ceiling boards go vertically?" I pointed out. Taking the photo, I showed Luis the direction of the ceiling boards in the image. "If that's the same ceiling as in the pic, then the boards end at the wall this way, butting up against the mosaic. So, it's not behind this wall. It's behind *this* one." I pointed to the wall behind the bed. "Help me move this."

"Damn. Good catch," Luis laughed.

Together, we heaved the wooden bed frame aside and ran our hands along the wall. Luis knocked on it and tried stabbing another screw into the plaster, but it needed an exposed section like the crack we'd started with. "Ellie, we're never going to chip this off with a screw. Let me go find a hammer or a pick-axe or something."

"I'll go with you. There's a shed in the backyard. Maybe there's tools in there."

"Or dead bodies."

"Not funny."

We went outdoors in search of the toolshed, only to hear Syndia berating Nottie for not being spry enough to help her carry planks of wood. "After this storm passes, we have to reconsider your employment. Now that my mother is no longer your concern."

"Ms. Duarte, I have nowhere else to go. I can earn my keep in other ways. Cleaning the house or maintaining the garden maybe?"

"I have nothing to pay you. Besides, you're no spring chicken anymore. You're pretty much useless to me now." Syndia was so damn careless when she talked to Nottie. What made her think she could just insult a woman like that? A woman *older* than she was?

Luis and I tried to circumvent Syndia, but she spotted us. Hands on hips, she gestured with her chin. "Only one more window to go. It's the large one in the atrium. Should I just cover it in tape?"

"No, I'll find something," Luis told Syndia. "Tape won't help."

"Well, find it quick, because this storm is starting." She scoffed before tying her hair into a tight bun that only accentuated the leathery wrinkles on her face. Behind her, Nottie watched us carefully, and I couldn't help but feel like she was asking for our help dealing with this crazed woman.

"Why tape?" I asked, still watching Nottie. Dark shapes flirted behind her, spoke to her, but she couldn't hear them. I blinked and focused on where I was stepping instead. Bacon ran in my way then trounced into the bushes.

"When there's no wood, covering a window in masking tape is the last option. Doesn't keep it from blowing in, but the tape holds the glass together so the pieces don't go flying everywhere."

I registered the wary look on Syndia's face as her gaze followed us through the garden, now that we were wandering toward her family's side of the yard. "There's no wood left anywhere if that's what you're looking for," she warned us then headed inside the house.

"What are we doing again?" I felt more lightheaded and disoriented than ever, the deeper we ventured into the wildest, untouched section of the property. Here, weeds grew as tall as my knees and even the moths wondered when was the last time they'd seen humans cross through.

"Looking for something we can use to chip away that wall," Luis said. "What's the deal with the mosaic anyway?"

"I think my grandfather made it. He made the mosaic table in that room too. There's an inscription on the underside to my grandmother."

"But I thought you were concerned about your missing key," he said.

"I was. I am. But I couldn't find it and then I saw those pics in a box. They must've taken them when they first bought my grandparents' house. It makes me sad that my grandmother couldn't take belongings with her, like that beautiful work of art."

"They must've taken a photo of it for posterity before covering it up."

"They should've just left it. It looked beautiful," I said. It didn't make sense. Had I bought a house and it came with a gorgeous handmade mosaic mural, I would've featured it, not covered it up.

"Where did you say that tool shed was again?" Luis wiped sweat from his brow. The humidity and fatigue was starting to get to him. I felt grateful to him for helping me out when he didn't have to.

"Over there." I pointed to the end of the seawall which disappeared into a thicket of mangroves. The water from the inlet sloshed into the tangled mess of roots, and the thick scent of rotting wood and algae infiltrated my nostrils.

"God knows the last time anybody came out this far," Luis said, pushing through denser and denser foliage. "You can tell she's had trouble taking care of this place."

"I know. See it there?" I pointed to the little house that finally broke through the greenery, there at the edge of the property. "Could be a toolshed."

"I think that's more like an old pump shed."

"Pump shed for what?"

"For a pool or something electrical that used to be out here. In fact..." His foot kicked at something hard underneath the fallen leaves and palm fronds.

Above us, the trees swayed in the storm front. I hugged myself in the now cool draft, just as the sun hid behind an overcast of clouds. "We should start wrapping this up. I'll find something to use for the wall, my nail scissors, a butter knife, anything."

"Wait, something's under here." Luis pushed at the ground with the toe of his sneaker and lifted up a corner. "It's plywood. Good, we can use this for her last window." He tugged at the corner of wood and lifted it out off the grass. Disturbed ants and centipedes crawled everywhere.

Luis indicated to the other end of the plywood, so I could lift it, but it was in fact three big sheets of plywood all laid on top of each other in sequential order to cover a large area. I helped him lift the first one so we could set it vertically against a palm tree. "There's a hole under there," he said.

The ground gave way to a concave, cemented bowl that was cracked and stained and hadn't been used in ages. "Looks like an old pool."

"Yep, that's exactly what it looks like." He crouched to stare into the dry basin filled with leaves and uneven layers of porous concrete. "Looks like they stopped using it long ago and have been filling it up with concrete."

"It's a weird place for a swimming pool," I said. "The corner of the yard."

"Maybe it was centered back when it was one property, but when they added more land, it got forgotten here in the corner." Luis shook his head and surveyed the area. "So much wasted property. I wish I had the money to buy this place up and fix it up nice. I hate seeing all this go to waste."

"Me, too. Believe me." Especially since half of it used to belong to my family. I walked over to the little wooden house and tugged at the door knob. "It's locked," I said, tugging at the shaky door. I was sure if I just pulled at it hard enough, it would bust open.

Ellie, go.

If that was my grandmother asking me to leave, then I definitely had to know what was inside.

"You okay?" Luis looked at me with concern. "You don't look well when you're here, I have to say. You're a completely different person from when I met you in town."

I nodded absently. "There's energy here that doesn't sit well with me. I never thought I'd say that, but there it is." All this talk of energies and gut feelings and hallucinations had me feeling less like my old self but more like my *real* self than ever before.

He nodded with a sigh. "I feel it too. It's like whatever, or whoever, is here doesn't want us around."

I couldn't deny it anymore. The ghosts—yes, real ones—were everywhere. "But then, I feel good energy too, like my grandparents'." I hugged myself in the wind that was growing harder and cooler by the minute. "A battle between good and evil. It's all here, and I feel like I'm at the center of it."

I was saying too much. I sounded crazy, but then again, if anyone would get it, it'd be Luis. He smiled and rested his shoe against the pump shed door. "A healthy skeptic, huh? Sounds like you knew more than you let on before."

"Hey, I was trying to stay sane before, okay?" I chuckled. Now, there was no point. The only way to get to the bottom of all this was to proceed full force, full crazy, and see where it all led.

"We're all going insane, Ellie," Luis said, reaching for the door handle, getting ready to pull. "Some just get there faster than others."

Then, he yanked—hard.

And when he did, his hand slipped off the handle. So did his other foot. And for a moment, I saw the darkness, the shadow people, heard the grunt, but it hadn't come from Luis. It came from something else, something hidden in plain sight, something just beyond the invisible veil. The entities protecting this corner were watching. It wanted Luis—us—dead. I saw the hatred, the anger, the ghastly offense that we were trespassing in this forsaken corner of the yard as a sheen of black energy washed over Luis's entire body.

Backwards, he slid into the hole that was the old pool…

…slamming his neck on the sharp edge of the other sheet of plywood laid down.

The raw-cut jagged edge severed his neck. His head snapped backwards like a PEZ candy dispenser yawning open, and Luis tumbled into the abandoned pit, blood pooling all around him, spreading into the bumpy ridges of the uneven concrete like spidery veins. His gaze looked up at me for help, but it was too late.

The light had gone from his eyes.

SEVENTEEN

I screamed.

No birds scattered. No cries echoed.

The heavy greenery absorbed all sound. Nothing stopped for me or Luis, yet everything had changed in an instant. One moment he'd been speaking to me, and the next, his body was broken inside a hole in the ground. I tore my gaze away from his helpless, confused stare, a vision that would haunt me the rest of my life.

"Shit…" I pulled out my phone to call 911, but for the life of me, I didn't know how to dial, how to log in with my thumbprint, how to anything. I couldn't think. I could only hear the sound of him gasping as he fell, heard the crack of his neck as it hit the plywood.

"What happened?" Syndia arrived at my side out of breath, hammer still in her hand. Her and her damn hammer. She spotted Luis's lifeless body and didn't so much as gasp or cover her mouth. She stared at it expressionless, inhaling a slow breath. "It was his own fault."

My head whipped toward her. "How could you say that? What the hell is wrong with you?" I wanted to push her into the pool to see how she'd like it and had to bargain with myself not to. "Why do you have an empty pool back here for your guests to fall into anyway?" I shouted.

"I told him not to go back here. I told him it was dangerous," she insisted.

"That doesn't mean he deserved it!" I sounded wild and irrational, though I was the normal one, yet nothing felt normal or ever would again. "God damn it!"

I had to pull myself together long enough to make a phone call. There was some trick to this—pressing the side button, holding down the home button, some shortcut for calling emergency services. I couldn't think of it. My brain simply wouldn't compute. I sank to the ground and rocked myself in a heap. "Jesus...think, Ellie."

"Don't call. He's beyond help," Syndia muttered.

"I still have to call," I growled at her. "We can't leave him here like this."

"The storm is coming in. Emergency won't respond 'til it's over."

"We still have to call," I insisted.

She remained quiet a moment, long enough to remind myself how to dial 911. I was two numbers in when my phone screen shattered in my hand, as Syndia's hammer came down and busted it into a million pieces.

"Are you kidding me?" I shot up and pushed the woman backwards. She stumbled into Nottie's arms, and they both looked at me like I was the insane one. "Why would you do that?" My chest felt like it was imploding, like I'd never take in a full breath again.

"I told you not to call."

"I don't care what you told me, you crazy bitch!" I howled.

"Neither or you listened. If you're not careful, I'll do the same to you."

"What does that mean?" I shook with rage. "Are you threatening me, Syndia?"

I may not have been the start of any problems, but I would definitely end them with violent force if it came down to it. I was stressed and without my pills, and now was not the moment to toy with me.

Taking steps at me with her hammer, she slammed the butt of it into a palm tree, leaving two scars in the tree's flesh. "I told you both to leave," she hissed. "I warned you, but you both stayed. You're not taking what's mine, Whitaker."

"Are you insane?" I yelled. "Do you even hear yourself? You're out of your damn mind, you know that?"

"Of course, I know it. It's why I warned you. Believe it or not, I care."

"You care?" I laughed maniacally. "You just busted my phone, you're threatening me with a hammer, and I'm supposed to believe that you care? You only care about your delusions. If there was a treasure, your grandfather would've left it for you, and his spirit would've told you where it was. Which means you're bullshitting, Syndia. You can't hear him and you only let guests stay here in case they can. Face it, the treasure doesn't exist!"

My words hurt her as though I'd wielded them with daggers.

The rain began coming down in heavy sheets, creating little expanding circles in Luis's deep red blood. Soon, the pool would fill with water, yard debris, God only knew what else the storm would bring, and a precious soul would be covered like yesterday's garbage.

I had to leave La Concha, had to grab my things, and casually walk out of here. As much as I wanted to figure out my grandmother's past, it wasn't worth my life. I wasn't sure that Syndia would try to kill me, but judging from how empathetic she hadn't been just now, I couldn't take the chance.

Rushing past her and silent Nottie, I headed to my room. Not sure where I would go, but the police station sounded as good a place as any. I could tell them what happened, show my phone as proof of a crazed innkeeper over at La Concha Inn, and hope that they'd let me stay for the duration of the storm. A shelter would also take me in, but without a phone to find one in Maps, I'd have to walk in the emerging winds looking for one.

I entered my room, looking back to make sure Syndia wasn't following me. She and Nottie hung back at the scene, getting drenched and staring down into the pool at Luis's freshly dead body. I felt bad leaving him there, but there was nothing I could do for the moment. I couldn't believe I had just witnessed such a horrible death.

As soon as I entered my room, though, something hit me. A clear sense of déja-vu.

The anguish I felt came alive, and I had to pause to catch my breath. The energies were growing stronger. *The elements,* my grandmother's voice told me, *heighten your perception.*

I didn't want rain or wind heightening my perception. I didn't want to see or hear or feel any ghosts around me. I'd seen more than enough of my share since I'd arrived. I'd seen too damn much. All I wanted was to get out of here, get back on my meds, and go home. Yes, my mother had tried to warn me, but I never imagined that the danger would come from Syndia herself instead of the hurricane.

I sat on the edge of the bed, gripping my head.

I couldn't stop the visions from pummeling me.

Nana cried, rocked on the edge of the bed next to me. Was she real? I didn't know anymore, not that it mattered. Her thoughts were my own... How would she live without her love? How would her baby grow up without a father? She'd become one of those widowed young women who few would take pity on. They would say she deserved it. She'd have to fend for herself, work two jobs, but those weren't the worst parts. The worst parts would be the lonely nights without Bill. She'd never marry again, never love again…

"Stop." I gripped my temples.

Cold energy shifted all around me. I heard the rain outside, but I also heard the pounding of my heart, my grandmother's heart, something rhythmic. My grandmother rocked some more, then stood up to scream at the night sky. Yes, it was nighttime outside in this waking daydream. The room filled with sweet scents of rain.

I was dreaming. Hallucinating again. None of this was real.

He wouldn't have left me, she kept saying. *He wouldn't have…*

"They killed him, Nana. They killed him on his way home to you. They took his Spanish gold then used the money to buy you out. It was a shitty thing, but it wasn't his fault," I told her. "There was nothing you could do."

They took what was ours. He never had the chance…

"What chance?" I asked.

He never saw the gold.

A hallucination talking back to me in real-time? Could Nana hear me in 1951? What did she mean he never saw the gold? How else would they have gotten a hold of it? He was the treasure hunter, the adventure seeker of the family. McCardle could only pilot a ferry back and forth along one route, and apparently pirate innocent lobster fishermen.

The pounding in my head grew louder. I screamed to release myself from it.

The vision disappeared but something else replaced it—pounding at the door.

"Who is it?" I called. The police? Syndia, asking to be let in? I couldn't piece together the fragments of dreams and reality fast enough, until it dawned on me. The pounding was hammering and drilling coming from outside while I'd been in a trance.

"No. No!"

Rushing the door, I yanked at the knob only to find it wouldn't budge. In the middle of the wooden door, several screws had been pushed through. The edges where light would've bled in were dark, and I knew she'd covered the door with the piece of plywood Luis had found. Underneath the door, shadows moved back and forth under the rain.

"Let me out!" I banged on the door, my palms turning bright red. "Let me out of here! You can't do this!"

"I can't let you out yet, Whitaker. I can't trust you. I'll let you out once the storm is over."

"Let me out now! I don't have any food or water. You can't do this."

"Drink water from the faucets. You'll be fine." Her footsteps disappeared down the hall.

My heart—I thought it would collapse from the stress this bitch was causing me. This couldn't be happening. She had trapped me in here and all I had were my things, a bed, an empty dresser and my own messed-up situation. No phone, no food, and Hurricane Mara about to hit.

Freakin' great.

Pulling out one of the empty drawers, I heaved it at the door but it only bounced off, causing dents and scratches. I lifted it and tried again, this time opening up the wood shutters and aiming it at the windows, already secured with storm plywood outside. I threw the drawer, cracking the window. All the good that would do me with planks of wood covering it.

One of the drawer's ends split into shards.

"My god, this isn't happening." What would I do for two days inside this room, assuming Syndia would ever let me out? What if something happened to her during the storm and no one would find me here for days? Weeks? Months?

"Nana, Mayai..." I picked up the side lamp and was about to throw it when I realized I'd be breaking my only source of light in this room. I put the lamp back on the nightstand like a good girl.

I had to calm down, or the anxiety would eat me alive. I needed my medicine. I didn't care what Mayai told me about connecting better without them. I wasn't built to be this psychic. I couldn't handle it.

Pacing back and forth, I knocked things to the floor and punched at the mattress to relieve anguish. Searching through my purse, I hoped to find a loose Zoloft somewhere, but only found a headache pill so I swallowed it back dry. The pressure in my temples would form a migraine soon, and the growing low air pressure outside wasn't helping.

I stared at the space where Luis and I had tried chipping away plaster earlier this afternoon. Now he lay dead at the bottom of a pool. A hazardous hole in the middle of the yard. I doubted this establishment ever had their licenses to begin with. Nothing to do but wait for the inevitable. My first hurricane and I'd be spending it as a prisoner.

I could cry about it, or I could keep tearing apart this wall.

Pulling out another drawer, I aimed the corner of it

into the wall and slammed it. A tiny chunk of plaster chipped off. I slammed the drawer again in the same spot. More plaster chipped off. Again and again, I used the drawer as blunt force, chipping away at the same spot until eventually, about an inch depth of plaster was gone. Underneath, light blue glass shone through.

My fingertip confirmed it—smooth tile.

The mosaic was there, just underneath the surface. It would take me forever to expose it without the right tools. Luckily, a storm outside began rolling in, I was locked in Room 3 for the foreseeable future with nothing better to do, except chip away at a wall to quiet my raging mind.

A meow startled me. I whirled around to find Bacon sitting up, eyes squinting.

"How did you get in here?" Demanding info from a cat—a new low.

I knew for a fact he'd been outside before Luis had slipped and fallen in the pool. I knew for a fact he hadn't followed me in here. He wasn't a ghost. He was real and solid and made of cat parts, so how...the hell...did he get in this room? I had no idea but I did know one thing—if he'd found his way in, that meant there was a way out.

EIGHTEEN

The good news was that there seemed to be a draft coming from the hole in the wall. The hole behind the safe where I'd found my grandmother's photos. The space probably led deep enough that Bacon used it as a passageway to get through the property, but the bad news was that I wasn't cat-sized and would never fit.

More bad news…

If I couldn't find the tools to help me chip away at this wall, then I'd definitely never be able to bust open Bacon's hidden space. I stood in the middle of the room, taking stock, trying to figure out what to do. It all felt so helpless, and my doom-and-gloom brain wasn't helping. Thoughts attacked me—I would die in here, this was my own fault, I was here because of how stupid I was…

"Stop, Ellie, stop!" I chastised myself.

Outside, the wind picked up, wooing and whistling all over the house. Loose debris flying around scraped the walls and windows, while I tried not to think about how much worse it would soon get.

I took inventory of what I had—not much.

But there *was* a bed, and the bed had a metal frame. With the screw Luis and I had used earlier before he was so freakishly killed by happenstance, I worked to unscrew the bolts holding the frame together. I didn't need to take the whole thing apart, only one long side and that meant five screws, two on either end, and one in the middle bolting down the crossbar.

Just loosening those screws took up two or so hours, and in that time, I cut my fingers into bloody shreds. During that time, what little light filtered into the boarded up house lessened even more, and I turned on the lamp to keep from being in total darkness. Whatever I meant to accomplish, I had little time to do it before the power eventually cut. Pulling out the last screw from the bed frame, I pulled apart the metal piece and held it up.

Like a spear or javelin, it felt weighty and solid in my hand. I wanted to wield it, smash everything in the room—smash Syndia's face if I had to. It was my only weapon in case I needed it. For the moment, however, I rammed it against the wall, over and over again, until the plaster began falling off in chunks, exposing more and more of the colored tile.

As I chipped away, building a rhythm, I fell into a trance.

With little light, all this repetitive motion served to put me in an altered state of mind. Soon, I was hearing voices, as I chipped away plaster. I heard my grandfather's deep voice talking to my grandmother. I heard her laughing and felt him taking her into his arms and kissing her.

Today's the day, Leanne, I can feel it.

Don't go, I heard her thoughts. *Something terrible's going to happen.*

"What happened, guys? Tell me what happened," I muttered.

Light blue tiles turned to medium blues and dark blues. Sometimes, I'd expose a green tile, sometimes white. Sometimes I'd accidentally chip a piece of tile and curse out loud for having damaged it. Eventually, at what might've been one or two in the morning, the entire Florida Straits came into view on the wall. The keys were represented by their own green tiles, and Cuba was comprised of a large dark and light green shape that resembled a hammerhead shark.

Why would my grandfather make his map this way? Why not draw or paint it on paper or canvas like a normal person would? Why make a map at all? Wasn't the information safer locked away in his head?

To manifest…

It was Maya's voice, echoing from a faraway place.

"Manifest? What does that mean?" I asked but got no response. Only more whistling wind and shaking shutters. A darkness seeped into the room that enveloped me like tangled arms of energy. "I hate ghosts," I muttered.

On the map, Northwest of Havana, between Key West and Cuba, was a swirl of white mosaic tiles. It almost looked like a little hurricane right in the middle, but I understood the symbolism. X marked the spot. Bill hadn't made it obvious with a big red X like in pirate movies, but the swirl got tighter with smaller, tinier bits of glass tile, and I knew this was his sweet spot.

The location of the Spanish galleon.

Grabbing my makeup brushes from my suitcase, I used the blush brush to clean away plaster dust from the tiles. The piece was extraordinarily beautiful, and when I put the little table next to it, I saw what he'd done. The table was a closer version of the swirl design, like someone had zoomed in by pinching out on their phone. Watery swirls, fish, and sharks appeared in on the table version. Details, closer-up.

I hadn't exposed the entire map, only enough to admire it in the feeble lamplight. *Why, though?* I kept wondering. All I could imagine was that my grandfather had been a visual person, an artist at heart. And like many of my middle graders in math, he had to create art with his visions in order to see concepts better in his mind. Maybe this wall mosaic had been my grandfather's vision board, a place to see his dreams clearly.

It humbled me to know that Bill Drudge had stood here some seventy years before and created this masterpiece right in this very room. It pained me to know that Nana couldn't take any of his art with her, that I had to stand here uncovering what time had so ruthlessly tried to erase.

"I'm sorry, Nana. You had to leave it all behind. That must've been so difficult for you." What an unfair start at life. I wished she was here so I could hug her and tell her how much I admired her for starting over with my mother, for living out the best remainder of her life as she could. Because of her, I'd had a good life.

The more I brushed away the debris, the more I could see what was underneath the tile. There was no need to chip the pieces away, since they were made of glass and clear. Right above the tight swirl was faint handwriting on the wall. A set of numbers—N 23° 54' 27", W 83° 37' 54".

Latitude and longitude.

Coordinates?

Coordinates my grandfather felt would lead him to the location of the Spanish galleon. How did one figure that out in 1951 anyway? With no internet, no computer models to help him? That took serious research skills. Even the *Titanic* hadn't been found for another thirty years.

Quickly, I reached for the photos I'd found earlier and shuffled through them. One was a close-up of this exact spot. Who took these pics? A pang of anxiety hit my chest, and I closed my eyes to try and see past the aggravation building in my body, see the answers in my mind.

Open up and access my intuition?

Okay, Mayai, you win.

I'd try it again. I envisioned it, the very moment in time these photos were taken, but it wasn't Bill or Nana who'd taken them. It'd been McCardle's wife—Susannah. Had she broken into their house and taken these photos while they weren't home? Or had Nana invited her in for a margarita…meanwhile, she'd snuck in to take a photo of their private bedroom wall?

I hated the uncertainty.

Bill never saw the gold, because he was cut off at the pass. The next door neighbors had the coordinates to his location. Good ol' Captain McCardle had gone off course to find the spot the same night my grandfather had headed out. Intercepted at sea.

Pirates abounded in 1951. And one of them had been Robert McCardle.

Holy shit, this hadn't just been a case of them finding my grandfather on the way back from his expedition and stealing his gold. No, this had been pre-meditated from the very beginning. They met him at the site.

N 23° 54' 27", W 83° 37' 54"

"Bastard," I mumbled.

I shuddered when the windows began wheezing, gasping for breath. Maybe I shouldn't speak to anger the spirits, considering I was trapped inside a room at the mercy of nature and the paranormal world.

But why the hatred? All because my grandmother had been different? Because she'd been a saucy woman unlike the pious ones who'd lined up to receive communion every Sunday? Because she thought for herself? Did they really want them out of the neighborhood that badly?

It was unfair and infuriating. I sat and admired the mosaic a long time, taking it in, imagining myself in their time. As the only connection to my grandfather, the piece of art felt like a responsibility for me to absorb. I hated the fact that I couldn't take a photo of it now that Psycho Bitch had smashed it with her hammer of deceit.

Outside, the storm had finally arrived.

All my life, I'd thought hurricanes were like tornadoes, beginning forcefully and suddenly. Instead, they crept in slowly, beginning as sunny days, then raining just a little, then a little more until the winds were howling over the roofs, and the planks of wood stuck to the windows rattled with fury. A slow deterioration.

Much like my sanity.

A flash of lightning illuminated the room for a bright moment. I saw the shape of a human shadow in the corner of the room. Someone was in here with me. I scanned the room, waiting for the next flash. On my suitcase, Bacon slept soundly curled up into a ball.

"How can you sleep through this?" I dropped my head against my knees, willing the spirits away. "Please, stop. Enough for one day."

There is nothing in here with me.

There are no ghosts.

It's all in your mind, Ellie.

In my heart, I knew it wasn't true, but I had to tell myself lies if I was going to make it through the night. I crawled into bed, now a mattress on the floor. I collapsed from sheer exhaustion. Each time the lightning flashed, I closed my eyes and imagined the storm going away, imagined the shadows moving to gang up on Syndia instead. But no matter what, I felt them nearby. Someone was haunting me.

"Leave me alone, leave me alone..." I chanted the mantra.

From the scraping, creaking noises outside, the sheer force of the hurricane's winds, and the house trembling with fury, I knew it'd be a while before I saw sunlight again. I may as well try to sleep through it. Perhaps in the morning, it will have passed and all this will have seemed like a dream.

A fucked-up, OCD-infested dream.

I flipped over and covered my head with the sheets like I had as a child when the visions attacked me. A moment later, something jumped up onto the bed, and I flinched, but it was only Bacon wanting warmth. I'd never been a cat person, but I could share the bed with him. After all, he'd led me to the photos and come back to keep me company.

Bacon is my lifeline, I thought.

Within seconds, I fell asleep and was aware of it. I could hear myself snoring and just didn't care to move or switch positions, I was so tired. I dreamed of Luis, trying desperately to pry open that shed door, slipping backwards and falling into the pool. I saw the moment he split his neck open in dreadful slow motion. I heard my own scream and told myself to imagine him as happy in heaven instead, if such a thing even existed.

Lucid, Mayai's voice slithered in.

Lucid dreaming, yes. I'm keenly aware of the changes in my psyche now that you've made me toss my medication into the ocean, Mayai. Thank you.

But in my dream, lucid or not, when Luis landed in the pool, he laughed and got back up. He chuckled and fixed his neck long enough to crawl out of the hole without his head snapping off completely. *It's here,* he said once he'd crawled out, shaken off the dirty leaves, pointing to the shed.

"What is?" I was scared to get near the walking, talking dead man.

The answers. He pointed to the lock, pulled the missing brass key from his pocket, and opened the shed's lock.

Wait. Did he have the key all along? Pulling the shed door back, he showed me the inside of the shed. The stains of caked blood on the floor, the flies laying maggots on the piles of flesh. The shed was floor-to-ceiling filled with dead bodies, and the freshest one on top...was me.

NINETEEN

The house roared like a freight train.

I awoke with a start to find the windows and walls shaking. If the house lifted and carried me into the sky right now, it would've been just as well. A exciting end to an otherwise boring life. Thank you, Key West.

Hurricanes weren't full of rain and lightning like I'd imagined most of my life. They were blasts of wind interrupted by even stronger blasts of wind. Gales piled upon more gales, a constant barrage I thought would never end. For hours, I'd been sleeping. For hours, I'd been hearing the atmospheric train running over the roof in my lucid dreams.

Luis, the key, the shed out in the back...

I couldn't check on any of it.

Stay inside...

Yes, I intended to. Thank you, spirits of the Ellieworld.

Bacon was gone. Probably headed back into his hiding spot. I'd hide there too if I was him. One of the articles I'd read last week mentioned how the safest spots during a hurricane were inside windowless framed rooms, like closets and bathrooms. If worse came to worst, I could hide in the bathroom and put this mattress over my head.

I would survive this.

But first, I had to survive my own mind.

Something sat on the bed with me. Nobody was there, but I could feel it, a female presence. I felt her anguish without having to see her and knew it was my grandmother. Still, I bristled, not liking the feeling of being with someone I couldn't see. In front of the bed appeared a woman. Angry lines, hair in curlers, a handkerchief tied around them. She spoke through the chain link fence.

I saw you posing in your little whore's outfit, Leanne. Through the window last night. Bob saw it too. You go around tempting the whole neighborhood husbands that way? Little tart.

Susannah, Robert's wife. My grandmother hated her, yet she couldn't stop her from harassing on a daily basis. I was pissed for Nana and wanted to tear those curlers out of her head and shove them down her throat.

You're going to pay for it, Susannah said, plucking weeds from the fence line that had crossed over from my grandparents' yard. She shook them at Nana. *Go to church and be saved, witch.* Then, she tossed the weeds back over, as they landed at my grandmother's feet.

The woman disappeared, leaving behind a cloud of disappointment on the bed. "You *were* better off leaving town. Sounds like nobody understood you here anyway."

Bill did. Bill understood me like no other.

When I blinked, it wasn't my grandmother on the bed with me but Mayai, turning to look at me over his shoulder. *Fight for her,* he said.

How could I?

I broke into tears. I was stuck in a cage, a storm raged on outside, and there was nobody left to help me. The only other person in the house was more insane in the brain than I'd ever imagined, a woman on the brink of losing it all. I'd been there too when I lost my boyfriend and my grandmother in the same night.

So had my grandmother.

So had Bill. So had my mother when she went through her divorce.

We'd all been on that brink before, where the world feels about to end but suddenly the clouds break and a silver lining appears. But not all of us went around with a hammer threatening to take others down with us. Syndia, though, was special. Lucky me.

The walls shook again, and for the first time since the storm started, I felt nervous and scared for my life. Luis had said that Key West had endured a lot of storms over the years and came out just fine, but no house on the island had looked as dilapidated as this one. I felt the structure was about to be compromised at any moment.

Maybe I'd overlooked this. Maybe I'd trusted my instincts too deeply, and now it was too late.

I laid myself down and tried going back to sleep, listening to the winds pummel the house, debris flying all around, windows getting hit with loose projectiles. Something slammed into the wall behind me, and I flinched.

"God, Universe, whatever you are...I promise to believe if you just get me through this bullshit," I bargained with anyone who would listen. Reaching over, I tried clicking on the light only to find that the power was out. Must've gone out a while ago as I slept.

The room filled with overpowering energies, like a surge of electricity before a lightning hit.

Just then, the corner of the ceiling lifted, nails ripped out of wooden beams.

"Oh, hell no." Please tell me the roof wasn't about to come off. I climbed off the bed and dragged the mattress into the bathroom alcove where the sinks were, taking the metal bar with me just in case. It was my only implement. Crouching under the mattress, I pulled it over my head and thought about my life. About everything it had meant and everything I still wanted to do.

Nails squeaked, wood creaked until suddenly, there was a pop and the room filled with 140 mph winds. I screamed and held the mattress close to me, using its handle, but the walls around me weren't close enough to hold it in place, and it yanked out of my hands and through the ceiling. I watched the roof yawn open some more, as the palms outside bent to the wind's will.

"Christ…" Using the metal bar, I slammed against the cat's hideaway opening over and over until big chunks of wall came loose. Enough that I could stick my hands inside and rip off big pieces of drywall. Once I'd exposed a big enough hole, I stepped over the safe bolted into the floor and crawled on my hands and knees, ignoring the spider webs and critters scattering at my presence.

Inside the space, I felt safer with all the internal structure and beams around me, but the opening I'd carved still gave the wind a place to blow into. That greedy wind. Didn't it have enough places to invade? The ghosts were nothing now, merely guides and wisps of the past.

I thought of my mother, of all the times she'd sat on my bed and felt my forehead for fevers. Of all the times she'd driven to school to bring me projects I'd forgotten, lunchboxes left behind. All she'd wanted was for me to come home, but I'd been too stubborn.

Now here I was with Mother Nature banging on my door and a crazy woman in another room who didn't care if I lived or died. Who would just as soon leave me outside to rot in a dry concrete pool and threaten anyone who tried getting help for me.

Somewhere outside this wall space, in Room 3, another piece of roof ripped off. I heard it tear then fly away. The only good thing was that its absence let in the tiniest bit of light. Even during a hurricane, sunrise still came. The sun stopped for nobody, no storm. No rays of sunshine invaded, but a dull, cloudy grayness gave me enough light to see that I wasn't just in a wall space but a passageway. And not just big enough for a cat but for a crawling human.

All around me...were things.

Books, boxes, papers bound with rubber bands, drawings of maps, more photos of my grandmother in the nude, plus a big leather book. Using my toe to reach it, I dragged it toward me and opened it. Her handwriting filled the moldy pages. Drawings of herbs, descriptions of their medicinal properties, the garden she was planning to create, a moon sculpture she wanted right in the middle. Next to it, a postscript explaining how Bill had made it for her from leftover coquina in the neighbor's junk pile, how marvelous the universe was that when she asked for something, it gave it to her.

Pages and pages filled with gratitude about her life, her wonderful husband, the beautiful little girl they'd had in later pages. It'd all been here for seventy years. A secret storage room my grandfather had built to keep prying and judgmental eyes away from his family. He'd thought of it all—the location of a Spanish galleon, how to keep his wife happy, how to protect her.

It was a shame he couldn't protect himself.

For the next several hours, as the storm destroyed the world outside, I sat cross-legged in this private space, surrounded by the energies of the people I loved. *Thank you, Bacon.* Thank you, roof ripping off, or I'd never have dug deeper.

My grandmother's book was called a "book of shadows," and it contained everything she knew at the time—about herbs, yes, but also about crystals, their uses, and their properties. Apparently, she put out rose quartz, carnelian, and red jasper every time she wanted to make love with my grandfather and she gave him black obsidian to carry in his pocket each time he went out to sea.

In the last pages, I felt her anger at how some of these things hadn't worked or he'd still be here with her today. She questioned her abilities and started doubting what she had always thought to be true. And then she said something that made me stop—would her daughter have the same abilities? Would she even want to teach them to her for fear of the same persecution? She wasn't sure. If Mariel showed an interest in the occult, she'd warn her of the dark sides. If she was inclined to learn the ways, then she'd assist her, but she wouldn't insist upon it. She'd let her be who she was, witch-inclined or not. Same for any grandchildren she'd have in the future.

Witch-inclined.

My grandmother really had considered herself a witch?

What did that make *me?*

With all my hallucinations and abilities to perceive energy around me, did it run in me as well? "Nana, am I one, too?" I asked aloud. If that was the case, what was I doing here inside a wall space hiding from a storm? I felt so filled with pride, I wanted to walk outside and harness the gales, toss them back to sea, but I wasn't a sorceress, for crissake. A witch was something else.

It meant making things happen, knowing what others didn't know. It was a natural inclination that everyone had, but only a few bothered to cultivate it. Maybe I had that inclination stronger than others.

If Syndia thought I wasn't here to take what was hers, lurking around every corner with her skull-bashing hammer, she was sorely mistaken. Guess what, I *was* here to take it. I would find that treasure. Like Mayai had said, it was time and I would fight for what had been taken.

And the moment this storm was over, that was exactly what I intended to do.

TWENTY

Mara was massive. And relentless.

Every time I thought a break in the action might come, she'd pick up again. Worse, the passageway had begun to flood, thanks to the roof flying off out in the room, so my ass sat in two inches of water. Wet, but safer here than there.

I moved deeper into the tunnel, away from the rising water, and I brought all my family's stuff with me. How would I get all these things out safely? If the hurricane didn't destroy them, Syndia would. Lying on a crossbeam inches off the ground, I put Nana's book of shadows, the photos, and my grandfather's papers on top of my stomach to keep them dry. Then, I listened to the winds, as I clutched the maps tight.

The passageway became a cocoon of whirling psychic energy.

Not only was I stuck here during a strong storm, but these items held long-lost vibrations that spread through me even just touching them. Soon, the rhythm of the winds had rocked me into another trance, and two days without my meds, I'd inevitably see the spirits again.

This time, it was I who traveled to where they were. I was transported to the ocean, a place I'd never been but could see with intense detail as though I'd grown up with it my whole life. The calm waters glistened under the evening sun, and the salt stung my burned cheeks and stubbled face. My boat, *Mariel's Luck*, bobbed up and down on this gorgeous twilight, as the orange ball of fire began sinking to the west. There was still plenty of light left, and I didn't want to go home without my prize. I wasn't me in this dream but someone else—I was Bill Drudge, and this was the last day of my life.

Nuestra Señora del Pilar was the lost Spanish galleon I'd been looking for the last seven years. It'd been part of a fleet of ten others traveling from Havana to Spain, bringing back untold riches, when they were blown off course by a deadly hurricane. The treasure was down there. I had tracked it over years of research.

N 23° 54' 27", W 83° 37' 54"

Those were the coordinates to my destiny. Leanne hadn't asked me not to go, but I could feel her trepidation. She'd slipped me the larger piece of obsidian. Earlier that evening, she'd talked in her sleep, begged me not to leave. But today was the day, I'd told her. I could feel it. Well, that much was true, only the day for what, exactly? A good day to die?

We located the ship and began the dive around noon. After hours of diving, we discovered layers of spilled gold underneath the sand and knew we'd hit the mother lode, but when we surfaced, another ship had met up with ours and our lookout, Martin, was dead on the stern.

The Havana Ferry—McCardle's vessel—empty of passengers.

What the hell was it doing here?

When I climbed up into *Mariel's Luck*, there he was waiting for me. The smug look on his face I'd remember for years to come. Even in death, you remember faces, smells, notes to memorable pieces of music. I told him there weren't no way in hell I'd hand the gold over to him after my years of diligent research, but then he threatened my wife. Said he knew where we lived, laughed, then looked at his co-captain. "She'll have no problem opening them pretty legs to me," he'd said. He'd seen her do it many times before through the bedroom window.

Didn't I know that was one of the reasons Susannah hated her so much? It was my fault, he told me. Mine and Leanne's, for being so obnoxiously in love. It made him horny and his wife resentful because of how often we did it. I could thank Leanne for what was about to happen, he'd told me, because his wife couldn't wait to get rid of us.

I seethed with rage.

I wanted to kill him, but I knew this was the end of the line. After trying to reach for his long knife, my fishing spear and pistol nowhere to be seen—tossed overboard, most likely—there was no way I could win this. I handed him the one bag we'd managed to bring up from the depths. "Promise me you won't hurt her," I said.

"Promise," he said then he twisted my body around and slit my throat.

Everything after that happened quickly. I'd moved into another dimension and watched it all unfold underneath me, as though from a higher plane. I was dead. I knew I was, but no way would I be moving on. I had to see what these bastards did with my gold and my woman. I had to make sure that she stayed safe.

McCardle's co-captain took my body back to the island in a motorboat while my neighbor piloted the ferry back to port. The motorboat arrived right at our home off the inlet where only Susannah witnessed my body and helped the sailor place it inside an empty shed. All the while, I could smell Leanne's cooking filtering through the kitchen screen—shrimp in garlic sauce—hear my baby's laughter, my wife's humming, while I could do nothing to reach them.

No worse agony than that.

McCardle declared the bag of gold with officials, claimed someone had left it behind, then went back a week later to my coordinates to dig up the rest of the *Pilar's* treasures. He'd used photos taken of my map, photos he'd sent his wife to go in and capture at my own home while my wife had been grocery shopping.

The man had everything he needed to take all that was mine. It'd been my own fault for making my visions into art.

Days later, my flesh was dismembered on the dock and fed to the fish, while my bones were placed in a pile next to that machine McCardle's son-in-law had invested in. I was ground up, just yards away from my clueless wife and child. Ground up and mixed in with shells and turned into a porous cement to be used for a garden wall. The circular garden wall that would serve as a center hub for the McCardles when they purchased my home. Just a few months later, their property had doubled in size.

The bitch had planned it for a while.

But Ellie, I was only the first victim of many.

Faux coquina had worked so well to get rid of evidence that Robert and his son-in-law went into the "disposing-of" business with mobsters returning from Havana on the ferry. For a small fee of several hundred dollars, they'd take the bodies off the criminals' hands, run the motorboat back to La Concha and make Spam out of the dead. Some of their clients were pretty big— Lucky Luciano and Meyer Lansky.

They made enough cash, between the rest of the galleon's gold and the blood money off these mobsters, to buy my woman out of our home. They expanded and made their own Camelot, but it wasn't meant to be, Ellie. It wasn't meant to be, because your grandmother employed her unique gifts that day and swore as she left, swore that prosperity and happiness of this family would never thrive.

I heard her the moment she uttered the words.

I helped her carry that intent to the Universe, Ellie, and whatever my woman spoke in those grief-stricken moments came true. That was why I loved her—she was fierce, brave, true to herself. And to be fair, McCardle stuck to his word.

He never did hurt Leanne.

The garden circle is lined with the bones of countless victims. And if you're not careful, you'll end up there too. Wake up. Wake up and forget this foolishness. You have your answers. I have my wife back. You need nothing else.

Water droplets fell on my face from a rafter above, as his voice dropped away into a dreamlike abyss. I sat up and gasped, sucking in lungs full of air, as the passageway filled with more pulsating wind.

I'd dreamed about my grandfather, finder of the Spanish galleon, *Nuestra Señora del Pilar*. His voice had been clear in my soul. When he'd felt the sun on his cheeks, I'd felt its heat. When he'd experienced elation at pulling up a bag full of gold doubloons, I'd felt the same. And when his heart had stopped upon seeing what awaited him on the decks of his ship, I'd felt it too.

"But is there hidden treasure, Grandpa?" I asked.

I needed him to tell me everything. "Is there?"

Yes.

I gasped. "Where? Please tell me where they put it."

The earth will tell.

"What does that mean?"

Our connection had gone. Of course, it had. I would have to return to the sleeplike state to hear him again. I'd have to hold his maps close to me again. I'd have to recreate the same atmospheric conditions again.

He'd given me the answers I'd wanted. He'd given them to me as a full-blown episode of my brain disorder. I'd never see OCD the same way again. What an amazing gift, this channeling of otherworldly energy. He'd done it so I would move on. So I could forget this place and not spend another second here. But what he didn't understand was that I wouldn't go yet.

I wasn't finished, and yes, Grandpa, I was damned stubborn—ask my mom.

If I'd stepped into a house of horrors, and Syndia was the current head of family business, I had things to finish. For Grandpa. For Nana. For Mom, too. Open the shed. Expose the revulsions that had happened here. Give coquina samples to police for DNA testing. I may have come to spread ashes, but that was almost a week ago.

Now that I knew the truth, I had a new mission—revenge.

TWENTY-ONE

I could alert police and have them begin an investigation into my grandparents' case. That would've been the sensible thing. Just walk out of here unscathed and present solid evidence. Problem was, all my evidence had come in the form of gut feelings, hallucinations, and dreams. They would lock me up in a mental institution before I'd ever see my grandfather's gold.

My other choice was to stay and fight. Bust apart the whole damn property like I'd done to this passageway. Clearly, Syndia hadn't wanted to go that far. She'd chosen to preserve the buildings as much as possible. That was understandable, since they were her livelihood, but what did I care?

When the wind finally seemed to slow down a bit, I ventured further down the passageway. Bacon had escaped through somewhere, I just had to find that exit. If the eye of the storm were going over us, then I should've been able to come out for air. But when I reached the end of the passage, I hit another wall.

"Where did you go, kitty?" I whispered.

As I'd left the area where the ripped roof had been, there was less light. I ran my hands along the walls and kept my ears open for any hints of where I was. Somewhere in the distance, a man was talking—a commercial, announcer's voice. A radio. Someone was listening to a battery-powered radio, and the weather man was explaining how the top recorded winds had been 150 mph at the eye wall, a Category 2 storm, and how the other half wasn't supposed to be as bad as the first. Only a few more hours to go, then they could assess the damage.

"Well, so far we're doing pretty good here," Syndia muttered. Her voice seemed to be coming from the dining room, and I guessed that this wall ended somewhere in the living room.

I jumped when suddenly, a section of the wall near the floor opened and Bacon popped through with a meow. A cat door. He'd stepped through an actual cat door I hadn't seen before with a plastic flap and everything. So this was how he navigated the walls. Unfortunately, I wouldn't be able to come out that cat door, especially not with Syndia standing there.

I decided to lie on my stomach to try and look through the cat door. This way, I could at least see what Syndia was up to and have an advantage over her.

"I think we're going to have some roof damage," she said, "but I can have that fixed as soon as I find the rest of the gold."

Who was she talking to? Nottie, I imagined.

Lifting the cat door ever so slightly, I peeped out and saw a lot of dust on the wooden floor, an area carpet and the side of the fireplace. Apparently, the cat door was in the corner of the living room. From here, I could also see all the plants the women had brought inside, a few legs of chairs, and Syndia's flip-flops stepping back and forth. She still held the hammer in her hand, letting it hang by her knee as she paced the floor.

"But I can't let you in on it, Nottie. I'm sorry but I can't," Syndia said. "I know some people would say I should share it with you. I mean, you are the one person who's stayed loyal to us when even my own sisters left me to fend for myself, but I can't. First of all, you're almost seventy. What would you do with that money? Second, how do I know you're not going to leave me in the dust and take off with the whole thing when I'm not looking, huh? How do I know you're not going to kill me?"

Syndia actually cackled, the first time I'd heard her really laugh, but what was more disturbing was that I couldn't hear Nottie's reply.

"I can't let that girl out either," Syndia added. "I knew she was after it the moment she stepped into this house. She only wants the truth. Pfft." She scoffed. "Yeah, okay." Dirty feet walked back and forth, stopping every so often so Syndia could presumably peek out through the boarded-up window's edges. "Then she brought that tour guide. That man had been here once before, if you remember. I should've taken him out when I had the chance. He's the worst out of all of them. You told him too much, and I nearly fired you there."

Taken him out?

The dead bodies in the shed came to mind, the ones from my dream with Luis. Was "taking them out" a regular thing for Syndia?

"I hated the way he knew so much. Why would you tell him about the ghosts and the machines?" Syndia asked. "Not smart, Nottie. But you never were the brightest crayon in the box."

Bacon meowed at me and purred. I pet his head and made no qualms when his wet saliva cheek rubbed across my hand, as much as it drove me crazy. The radio turned down slightly, and I had the feeling Syndia was listening.

"Shh," I told the cat and held my breath.

"The good thing about having strangers in the house,

though," Syndia added, "is that each one brings a different theory to the table. It's good to hear their view of things, as much as I hate having them here. Like the ghost guide. The ghost guide told a group of tourists once that there was a change in energy around the fountain. I don't know what that means, but maybe it's buried under there."

The gold buried under the fountain?

It would explain why McCardle's ghost had so vehemently protected that area yesterday. Though yesterday seemed like ages ago, at this point. The storm had dragged the hours out and made them seem so long.

"I just didn't want to dig there, because you know…my grandfather had it made for my grandmother. It'd be a shame to destroy it. God, why don't I just invite a metal-detecting crew to come in and find the damn thing then split it with them fifty-fifty?"

My stomach growled. It'd been almost two days since I'd eaten.

Syndia paused. Her feet paused. She took a few steps toward the cat door, while I shrank back. *Don't let her hear me in here.*

"Know what I mean, Nottie?"

Syndia would share the findings with a metal-detecting crew before she'd share it with her mother's faithful nurse? She crept closer to the fireplace. I held my breath and tried not to make a noise. A shadow came near the door and slowly, a woman's hand pushed its way in.

Syndia deposited something on the ground then pulled her hand back. The fleshy piece of meat she'd apparently given Bacon was bloody and made my stomach heave. Was that a tongue? It certainly looked like a human tongue.

Oh, God...

The bile in my stomach rose into my throat. What was more, Bacon actually sniffed it and licked the drops of blood, and for a moment, I changed my mind about the cat entirely and hated him with a passion, but then he turned his nose up and refused the fleshy lump.

I couldn't calm my heart anymore than I could stop my insides from recoiling. What was Syndia doing out there? I imagined a family where getting rid of human evidence was so prominent, such a way of life to them, it just didn't matter anymore what you did to anybody. There were no consequences when you got away with everything. No remorse when one could easily dispose of flesh in the inlet then grind the bones with your rock-pulping machine.

How sick were these people?

Murderers.

When she headed back to the dining room, I again pressed my eye against the crack in the cat door to see what else I could see. A metal bucket by one of the table's legs, and Syndia kept throwing something into it. Whatever it was sounded dull and fleshy. Then, I heard a thwack of something hitting the wooden table, and a hand, black and blue and indistinguishable, fell into the bucket.

I turned right around in the crawl space and threw up close to the ground. Great. Now she would hear me heaving, and I'd be next on her table. Was that Nottie's hand? What had that poor woman done to deserve this?

"Unfortunately, you heard that man mention the energy around the fountain, too, and that's why I had to yell at you. I'm so sorry." Another fleshy body part hit the bucket, and again, my stomach heaved. This time, I couldn't keep it quiet, and a gagging sound escaped my throat.

Bacon sniffed the vomit and recoiled like today was leftovers day at Camp La Concha. He pushed through the cat door and into the house in search of better fare.

Meanwhile, Syndia got down on her hands and knees, and I knew I was shit out of luck. Pushing her cheek close to the cat door so she could take a peek inside, I thought about punching her in the eye, but then she'd know for sure I was in here, and a shit show would ensue.

Apparently, she already knew because the next thing that happened was the butt end of the hammer smashed its way through the wall, opening up two gashes. Two slashes of light filtered in. I screamed and covered my mouth, but of course, that was a moot point.

"I know you're in there, little rat. Not taking what's mine. You hear? You'll die in there eventually." The hammer smashed through the wall again, but this time I took a chance and reached for it, clinging to it with my thumb and forefinger, pulling on it as hard as I could.

I'd pulled in the blunt side and was yanking on it with all my might, while Syndia pulled on the wooden handle with both hands. Our strengths were pretty even, but with my foot firmly pressed up against the wall, I was able to wrestle it away from her slippery, sweaty hands.

"Damn it," she said.

Great, I'd gotten her hammer. Not sure what I could do with a hammer, but at least I could go back to Room 3 and push nails out the opposite way with it. "You didn't have to go this far, Syndia," I told her. "We could've come to an agreement."

"There's nothing to agree on, Whitaker. Nobody takes what's ours. Whoever tries to becomes part of the masonry. It's that simple. This place is built on the souls of all who've trespassed here."

"Too bad I'm not a trespasser," I said, crawling back on my butt and hands. "I'm the one person who actually belongs here."

"Good, because you'll die here."

Grabbing something off the fireplace mantel, she pushed it into the crawl space and dumped it—a bottle of liquid onto the floor. I grabbed the notebook and papers and turned around to book it out of there. Then, striking a match, she tossed it inside and the whole puddle caught fire.

Searing heat engulfed the tunnel, and I bustled away on my hands and knees, avoiding flames which spread quickly, thanks to the airy draft coming from the hole in the wall. They licked at my feet and ignited the corners of my grandfather's papers.

I smacked them against the floor to put the fire out, but Syndia threw another bottle into the passageway and the whole thing began sizzling. Mosquito spray. She'd thrown a whole can of bug spray. Was there no end to this woman's insanity? As soon as the container began bubbling, I knew I only had seconds before it exploded.

I ran all the way to the end of the corridor, to the opening to Room 3 and jumped through with all the papers I could carry close to my chest. An explosion propelled me out and into the intense winds of Hurricane Mara. I gaped at the totally broken room. The roof had been completely torn off, only three walls left standing, leaving me with the challenge of holding onto something or risk being whisked away.

And another prospect entirely—no need for the hammer. I was free. Bad news—I had no shelter.

TWENTY-TWO

I was at the mercy of the elements.

The winds had died down, but they were still strong enough to flail me like a paper bag. Rain settled in, its windblown spiky drops piercing my face. Inside the naked shell of Room 3, I reached for a plastic bag that had blown in from somewhere and put my grandparents' papers and book of shadows in it. My nana's photos were in my purse, but I was sure that had blown out of the room hours ago.

Now I understood journalistic photos of hurricane victims after the storm, walking around, picking at the ground, looking for evidence of their lives in the strewn debris. I moved around the room, reaching for the next corner of the wall or armoire to hold onto. Opening a drawer to the armoire, I placed the plastic bag inside to protect it.

My next milestone would be the big center tree up ahead. If I could reach it without getting blown away, I could hold onto it. Sprinting towards it, I miscalculated the distance the wind would push me and ended up holding onto a palm tree instead. The palm tree was better, actually, not as wide a trunk and easier to wrap my arms around.

Standing outside during a hurricane, hugging a tree, I contemplated my existence. How had I ended up here?

Stubbornness, that's how. I had finally gotten outdoors, where tropical storm force winds were the better option over being anywhere near that psycho bitch and her house fire. The smoke carried away quickly, and the flames were dying down, but there was no doubt that the west half of La Concha Inn, my grandparents' half, would sustain significant damage.

From here, I could keep an eye on the back door in case Syndia came outside for me. Now that she'd killed Nottie, there was nothing to stop her from killing me too. Right now, I had to make it over to Luis somehow. If my dream was right, and he had the missing key, I had to take that back. I couldn't risk anyone—Syndia, the police, whoever would find this mess after the storm—getting it. It might not have opened anything important, but it had been important enough to steal.

I reached for the next palm tree, but it was just out of arm's reach. Taking the hammer hanging from my shorts, I used the butt end to reach it and claw the tree to pull myself forward. I did this for several more trees until I'd reached the far corner of the McCardle's yard. The remaining plywood left over the pool had blown away and the empty hole had filled with blown branches and vegetation.

Luis wasn't there.

I had to ignore the deep red stains mixed with the greenery and get down there to look for him.

The pool's depth worried me. Once I reached the bottom, how would I get back up? Luckily, many fallen branches served as bulk on which I could get leverage. The winds were still cranking but the lower I went into the pool, the less I felt the effects due to the pool walls blocking it. My hair whipped around my face, making it difficult to see what I was doing. After tossing several branches aside, I finally uncovered the bottom.

Still no Luis.

"Come on, come on…" I searched everywhere for a body and also the cement for a fallen key. "Damn it." Where had he gone? It wasn't like his wound was one he could've recovered from. The man had definitely been dead.

Frustrated, I climbed the tangled mess of branches and fallen tree trunks back out of the pool and crawled to the nearest palm tree to hold on. Had that key been for the shed, like in my dream, then I didn't need it when I had a hammer. Running over to the shed, I used the wall to block the winds blowing from the opposite side. The shed was more like a small concrete building at the end of the seawall on a solid, concrete foundation. Filled with dead bodies or not, it'd be a good shelter.

The door had an old padlock, but it didn't seem like the kind that would use such an old key. With the hammer, I struck the padlock several times but it wouldn't break off. I put my body weight into it, a hard thing to do when I was being slapped around by winds. I struck at the padlock again, over and over again until the hinges on the bolt came loose, then pulled at the door until the wind caught it and slammed it open all by itself. The shed was empty. Well, not totally empty, but it wasn't piled high with dead bodies.

Sometimes, dreams were just dreams.

I stepped in, closed the door and locked it. Inside, the air was stagnant and musty while outside, the wind crooned and whistled all around. In the center of the building was a long six-foot metal table, like a commercial kitchen table for preparing food, with fish scales littering the floor. It was some kind of cleaning station for bringing back the catch of the day and gutting it before taking it into the house. A hose was coiled off to one side, confirming that this was used for cleaning.

Water still dripped slowly from its valves like it'd been used recently.

Honestly, I was relieved beyond belief. It'd been the first normal thing I'd seen all day, but the moment I closed my eyes and exhaled a sigh, a vision from another place and time flashed through my mind. A freshly dead body lied on the table. All his clothes removed in a heap on the floor. A woman in older clothing was gutting him from chest to groin, eviscerating him completely, removing his organs one by one and feeding them to the fish through a hole in the corner.

She paused and looked at me—Syndia.

I shook my head, gasping for air. "No, no, no..." Why? Why must my brain show me such things? Something in the corner caught my attention. A small closed door in the floor leading to the inlet below. When I removed the latch and tugged on it, the wind whipped up underneath it and slammed it open. Forcefully, I closed it back up.

My heart pounded. This was where they tossed the flesh of their victims—the skin, the meat, the insides— anything that turtles and fish and alligators might love. The hose washed away all blood and bodily fluids, and right there, along the edge of the room was a gutter. I crouched low to examine it. More fish scales but also traces of hair. Brown hair, long hair, silver hair. Still wet with bits of flesh still attached.

Recent, not old.

I felt the rush of my stomach coming up again, but I'd had nothing to eat and dry-heaved instead. This room had been used for de-boning, for cleaning and preparing bodies. Same as butcher shops had done with chickens

175

and fish and livestock all across the world, except with victims over the last seventy years. Human victims.

When I blinked again, the dead man on the table turned his head to look at me with wide-open blue eyes. "Help me."

"No. Stop."

I couldn't stay here another minute. I didn't care if the wind was still going, I would've rather stayed outside than be locked in here with ghosts of a wretched past. It was then that I noticed the walls behind me covered in tools. Knives, some still dirty, some rusted, hand drills, and scoopers, the kind that looked like they were used to scrape the inside of a jack-o-lantern on Halloween.

A few spots were empty. Missing tools. Syndia was probably using them inside the house. Taking a last look at the room in case I had to answer questions during a homicide detective interview, I left the shed but not without going back in a second to pluck something off the wall—a large sharp boning knife.

A flash and the walls dripped with blood. I couldn't stomach anymore and shut my eyes against the vision.

I closed the door. I shoved the knife into my shorts' pocket, slicing through the back. The hammer went into the other pocket. Now all I had to do was get the hell out of here, report this house of violence to the police, and blow this shit wide open. Maybe even get back this house for my grandmother, so she could rest in peace.

So *I* could rest in peace.

But the wind had picked up again, and this time holding onto palm trees wasn't enough. My body got blown back and slammed into another tree, and while I was counting the stars in my head, a large piece of aluminum siding blew past, gashing my forehead. I cried out but held onto the tree. The reality of getting tossed around by a hurricane hit me hard.

I was going to die either way.

"Whitaker, where are you?" Syndia screamed into the wind. "You'll die out there."

She hadn't seen me lying here, but one scan across the property and she spotted me in the grass. Employing the same tree-hugging method, she jumped from palm to palm, bloody knife in her hand, pausing at one to gaze at me, checking to see if I were alive. She wore an apron covered in bloodstained handprints, and her wild hair flew all around her like Medusa.

"Come back inside," she said with a laugh then muttered, "before I lose you."

So she wasn't concerned for my safety; she merely didn't want to misplace my dead body in this tropical typhoon. Didn't want to miss the chance to add the Drudge granddaughter's bones to the family garden wall. Huh, Syndia?

"I can't move." I hoped the lie would get her closer to range. I crept my hand into my pocket, fingers at the ready.

"Good, that makes things easier for me," she said before charging at me.

I acted quickly, pulling out the knife and pointing its gleaming end at her, but the winds had shifted, knocking her off course. She landed on top of me. I felt no pain. She must've gotten her knife stuck somewhere behind me. My blade, however, penetrated her shoulder near the edge of her skin and pulled off a chunk of flesh. Howling in pain, she screamed obscenities, gray glassy eye bearing down on me.

For a moment, I almost felt like I'd seen her this way before—a long time ago. In one of my night terrors as a child. Her arched eyebrow and hateful gaze looking down at me in bed. In my dream, I had hid from her. Not anymore.

"You bitch," she growled.

"Right back atcha," I said, but then she got leverage and, despite Hurricane Mara, despite the flying trees and loose aluminum siding blowing over our heads, despite a million projectiles that could've stopped her, she managed to shove her bloody, dirty knife into my back.

TWENTY-THREE

Ellie, honey, you can let go.
It's alright.
Nana's voice.
I know you're doing this for me, but I'm happy. I'm back with Bill.

Thank you, love. Thank you for bringing me home. You can let go now. Come with us.

She wanted me to release myself of pain, to give into my fate.

Someone pulled me by the hair. Dragged me across a flooded yard. Water sloshed up my nose, sharp edges dug deeper into my wound, and that damn wind hadn't stopped yet. The storm. I was outside in the storm, and the pain in my back made me want to end it all.

But I dared not move.

She thought I was dying—Syndia. And maybe I was, which would explain why I faltered in and out of consciousness, why I couldn't move, even when my mind wanted to get up and fight. She dragged me all across the jagged property. Every so often, I'd crack open my eye and see her struggling, tugging me by both my feet. When she'd hit a rock or a pile of fallen leaves, she'd maneuver me around them. Why wouldn't she just take me back inside the house and wait for me to die there?

Because she was insane, that's why.

I had to stop trying to make sense of her actions—
there were none. Syndia Duarte was an obsessed woman
who'd lost it long ago, searching for her precious Holy
Grail when there was no one left in life to share it with. A
woman who'd lost touch with all reality and consequence.
And I was about to become another pile of pebbles in her
wall.

"I told you to leave, but no. Never tell me I didn't try,
Whitaker." She huffed and heaved my body over more
rocks and mini rivers that had formed during the storm.
"I tried. I definitely tried to protect you. But you insisted
on staying."

I groaned.

My fingers blindly felt around for my knife and
hammer, but my pockets were empty. I had no defense.
The best thing to do was keep pretending I was dead,
keep hearing Nana's voice comforting me, telling me it
was okay to die if dying was what I decided to do. But I
wasn't ready. I still had too much I wanted to do.

A new career in something, I didn't know what yet.

Talk to my mother, ask her all the questions I didn't
get to ask Nana, appreciate her.

Get married to someone maybe. Have kids of my
own and never, ever tell them that their visions weren't
real. I'd tell them their visions were evidence of their
power, and the sooner they started learning how to
harness it and use it, the better off they'd be. I'd wasted
so much time being afraid of mine. The ghosts were
awful but they couldn't hurt me.

This bitch, however, was a different story.

I knew where she was taking me—to the cutting
machine. I saw them all—Bill, Nana, Robert, Susannah,
even Mayai—spirits of the forest, all standing around the
clusters of trees in different positions, watching the scene

unfold.

Helplessly, they watched while Syndia finally got me over to the machine and threw my legs down in exhaustion. "Damn, you're heavy." She grunted then came the sound of two knives sharpening against each other.

Even if I could sit up now, I couldn't move. The sharp pain in my back made it difficult to breathe. Must've nicked my lung. My foot was lifted, and Syndia's thumb ran across the bones of my ankle. "Pretty feet, Whitaker." She laughed and fished around her pocket for something. "Ready to become cement?"

When she pulled the brass key out of her pocket, I almost shook my head. She'd taken it back herself? I moaned low and tried to push the radiating pain out of my body by imagining it not there.

You're healed. You're made of light.

The body is only a vessel.

Rise out of it, Ellie.

I'd heard my grandmother talk this way a few times over the years, but because I always waved it away as nonsense, she never pursued it. She simply assumed I was another skeptic and stopped banging me over the head with her spiritualism. Now I felt guilty that I hadn't listened or learned from the master.

You're the master, she said.

You're stronger than I ever was.

The wind knocked the key out of Syndia's hand and she squatted to pick it back up. "I keep copies of this key everywhere. This one was in your bag. You must've found it in the same place as that hole in the wall."

I couldn't reply, but my eyes were completely open now, my gaze on the monstrous dinosaur of metal where I'd had that horrible vision of legs being snapped off like wishbones. She followed my gaze. "Oh, this machine? You're right. They don't make 'em like this anymore. Fact, they don't make them at all."

She pushed the key into a slot, pulled on a lever, and a deep motor turned on, its rumblings resonating over us. It was the kind of machine they made in old days, when levers cranked, other parts whirred, and engines were loud enough to blow your eardrums out. A thing so sturdy not even hurricane-force winds could move it across the yard. An old, dependable beast, functional even in this weather.

"Usually, we clean you guys out first," she yelled over the noise. "Grinding is messy. But I think I'd like pink coquina this time. When I see it in the wall, I'll know it was you. You know, special." She laughed and held onto the machine while a particularly strong gust of wind blew in from the inlet.

Pink coquina. Did she mean...?

Yeah, she did. She meant that my blood and flesh would mix in with the bones and shells and create a unique blend of concrete. That *would* look pretty, but I had bad news for Syndia—she wouldn't be getting her faux pink coquina today.

Maya's voice echoed through my soul—*fight*.

She'd be getting stubborn-ass Ellie.

"Alright, let's get this going," she said, reaching for a bag of sand. Or were they shells? Yes, crushed shells.

When the wind died down again, I kicked up suddenly, wedging my foot deep into her crotch. She cried out in pain, hands gripping my foot, but I managed to wrestle it free and kicked her again. This time in the chin, knocking her backwards. Her shoulder hit against the beastly machine, but the wind was making accuracy difficult, and I didn't get the result I'd hoped for. I tried sitting up, blinding white pain radiating throughout my back.

For the life of me, I couldn't take in a full breath of air. Syndia came at me then to try and finished what she'd started, but I held her at arms' length.

Life slowly seeped from my soul.

Her body pressed down on my trembling arms so hard, I thought my elbows would snap. "Why...won't...you...die?" she screamed.

My lower body, at this point, was stronger than my top, so I hoisted both my feet under her and leg-pressed her skinny ass off of me. Her body went flying and again, she smashed into the machine, but this time I got up and grabbed a hold of her neck. Pushing her head down toward the whirring blades, I made her sweat. Behind her, she kicked out like a five-year-old learning to swim.

"Stop..." she demanded. "Please."

Yeah, that was sweet, watching those beads of sweat pool up on her hairline like that. But the bad thing about having both my hands on her neck was that the rest of her body was free, and in one of her wild swings, she grabbed a hold of my loose hair and yanked on it.

"Ah!" I cried out, as she pulled harder until my long hair was feeding into the blades. I smelled the motor, the burnt parts that hadn't been turned on in a while, the gasoline, and her sweaty armpits covered in dark stubble, as she held me firmly against her hip and pushed me into the machine. "Fuck you. I won't..." I pushed backwards against her. "Die...like this!"

Syndia was strong, but she was over fifty, and the nice thing about being twenty-six years old was that it didn't matter how often you worked out, your body was still newer and ready to work harder than it had all these years. I didn't know where the energy came from, but a boost of adrenaline shot through me, and I managed to push that skinny bag of bones back about five feet.

Grunting, I grabbed the boning knife on the floor and ran with it. No clue where I was headed but right now, I just needed to get away from her. I got about halfway across the property when Syndia appeared out of the outer hallway through a tangle of trees.

"Don't go near that fountain," she said, pointing her hammer at me. "Don't you dare."

I faced her, legs apart, blade in hand, ready for whatever came next. Gesturing to the fountain behind me, I shrugged. "What fountain? This fountain? Why not, Syndia?"

She fumed, blood covering her teeth.

"Because the treasure's buried there? Of course the treasure's buried there. You know why?" I challenged her. "Because your murderer grandfather didn't care for anyone else to have it. Because my grandmother made sure of that through her curse."

"Shut up, Whitaker."

"That's the thing about murderers, they're only in it for themselves. I mean, who does that? Who hides the family money from the *rest* of the family? Oh, wait, your grandfather did. See? No love between him and your grandma. No trust either."

She stepped over a fallen bush to reach me, but I backed into the garden and stood in front of the fountain. "Shut up. Shut up right now," she growled.

"Whereas my grandfather made things way too easy to find. He loved his wife *so* much, he left her a goddamn mosaic mural as big as an entire room proclaiming where she could find the gold in the event of his death. See, *their* gold."

"Leanne was a village whore and everybody knew it,"

she spat. "Don't try to kid yourself. She didn't love your grandfather—she loved everybody." She laughed, but I knew that wasn't true.

"That's the lie they told themselves to make it okay. To absolve themselves for their sins. Murdering the neighbor, covering the evidence up with that shed over there and with homemade cement, accepting cash once the mob found out about the family business." I stood behind the fountain and held onto it.

The winds picked up again. There was no end to this nightmare.

Behind me, the canopy of the massive banyan tree swayed. Palm trees were perfect for storms with their wispy tops and thin bodies, but banyans? I worried about its roots so close to the surface, about its top-heavy crown. It was a sail-laden galleon catching too much wind, waiting to be tipped over.

Another gust bore down on the island, as I held fast to the fountain while Syndia held onto a lamp post. There was no point in speaking now. She wouldn't hear me anyway. The wind screamed all around, and I closed my eyes. This was a good time to feel its power, the raw energy of Mother Nature herself. It fed me, healed me, and became one with me.

I accepted what I'd always known to be true—all my life, pills had been used to suppress me. That might've been my mother's fault but she hadn't known better. It wasn't meant to be then. Now was different. Now I had control. I knew I couldn't kill this woman the same way she was looking to kill me, but that didn't mean I couldn't turn it around.

Send her own energy back her way.

"I'll tell you why everybody hated Nana," I whispered, envisioning beautiful young Leanne in my

185

mind. "Because she was the real deal. Didn't give a damn. Didn't care if she was different. Didn't care if the whole town saw her as weird. If being independent and in actual love with your husband, if loving sex was a sin, unlike half those bitches back then, meant she was a witch, then yeah—guilty. They got rid of her because they envied her."

The tree behind me began to groan.

I listened to its lament and told it the same thing Nana had told me—*you can let go now. It's time to die. But don't let it happen in vain. Exchange death for truth and life will go on.* I'd never talked to a tree before, but this wasn't any ordinary tree. This tree knew things. It had watched me from the moment I'd arrived. For seventy years, it had flourished on the life force of the souls who lay here. This tree had seen it all and kept quiet when it had desperately wanted to speak.

This tree would speak now.

One last gust of wind rocked the island, and the whole banyan lunged, groaning as it slowly toppled. Massive tangles of vines and twisted, ropy roots ripped out of the ground, lifting into the air like the stern end of a sinking ship, and I watched the stone wall made of bone mortar, Grandpa's moon sculpture, concrete foundation, the fountain and everything that had been built over its massive network of roots rise into the air with it.

I threw myself at the ground to keep from being in its way and crawled to the side, collapsing against a palm tree. Syndia's gaze was fixated, horrified, on the destruction of her beloved homestead.

For a moment, the roots and its stone ornaments all hung suspended against the deepening evening sky like a demented Christmas tree. Then, growing heavier under its own weight, the stone particles collapsed, breaking apart and tumbling to the ground in massive, rocky chunks. Broken dreams. Broken souls. The fallen tree's giant roots exposed dark fertile soil, and something else—bags.

Canvas bags.

Dozens of them. Many had split open, their sparkling contents raining down into the yawning pit of earth. Gold. Spanish gold. The stolen, bloody gold of Bill Drudge, the best boat captain who ever lived.

TWENTY-FOUR

I'd said it several times.

I could still hear my voice inside my head—*I didn't come for the treasure. I came for the truth.* And that still held true. But there was no way I could let this woman take what my grandfather had worked so hard to achieve, his life's goal and dream, his gift to his family.

Not again.

I looked at Syndia's face and could see that she felt the same, that she hadn't worked so hard taking care of this rundown place only to let some newcomer take what was hers. But I wasn't a newcomer. Inside my soul inhabited every single one of my spirit guides—Mayai, my grandfather, Nana, even my mother lived a little bit inside of me—just like I would live a little bit inside my future children.

I'd hoped that Syndia would rush the gold, start picking up the pieces like candy on the ground after bashing a piñata. That way, I could use her distraction as a moment to my advantage. But instead she let out a scream to rival the freight train winds of Mara and came running at me. It was me or her for the gold, and only one of us would get it.

The survivor of the fight, I knew.

I ran with the boning knife, jumping over knocked down trees, heading for the edge of the property. The coquina seawall was there, disappearing into the mangroves. On the dock below, a neighbor's fishing boat had been displaced by the storm and lied sideways capsized against the shore. Next to it were two more boats knocked over like dominoes.

I jumped down onto the dock and sloshed through high water covering it to reach the boat. If I could push off just enough, I'd wade out into the inlet and Syndia wouldn't be able to reach me. Of course, it would be the old man and the sea at that point, but I would take my chances.

The hurricane winds had died down anyway having knocked down the banyan tree as its finale, and now only the rain remained. I could deal with rain. Rain wouldn't suck me into the sky.

I tried pushing the boat out, but it was heavier than I could've ever imagined. I jumped in anyway, hoping to find a gun or something I could use to stop Syndia, but she had already climbed in after me, limping as she dragged her dirty feet through the slick white fiberglass of the vessel.

"Go get your treasure," I called, sidestepping the cabin. "It's waiting for you."

"I will," she replied. "As soon as I don't have to worry about you anymore."

"That'll never happen. As long as you and I are both on this earth, you'll have to worry about me." Behind her, on the inside wall where I'd stepped aboard, was a fishing spear.

"That's why I'm going to fix that right now." She lunged at me over front glass of the wheelhouse and dug her claws into my upper arm.

With my blade, I jabbed against her hand, leaving her deep cut marks and a lot of pain, but she yanked back her hand, digging her nails into my skin as she pulled. I bit my lip to keep from crying out. I didn't want her thinking she had the upper hand in any way, shape, or form. Never in my life had I ever been in a physical fight, and now I'd been in a few all in one day.

She lunged at me again and knocked me off my feet onto my back. While she climbed on top of me and tried to smash my head in with her hammer, I held her wrists up in the air, keeping her hands at bay. Dropping her hammer on purpose, she let it fall, and I tried so hard to move in time, but it bashed my face.

I heard a distinctive crack. My field of vision turned deep purple with scattered yellow stars. I'd never felt pain like this in my life.

"I'm sorry." Her tone was sugary fake. "Did I break your nose?"

Once I'd regained my ability to see, I pushed her torso up high enough to let go of one hand and throw a punch into the middle of her face with the other. All in the same day, she'd tried lighting me on fire, stabbed me in the back, and pushed my head into a cutting/grinding machine.

My fist connected with her cheek.

Her hands flew to her face, and in that second, I rolled out from under her, running to the stern of the boat. My hands grasped the fishing spear, and while I tugged at it, trying to remove it from its bracket, Syndia yanked me down by my shirt. Between the unsteady rocking of the boat, the abating winds, and the rolling of the ocean waves, my feet slipped.

I rolled onto my stomach and reached for a loose life preserver floating around a foot of salt water. As I reached for it, she tugged at my kicking legs, and I swiveled to slap her along the side of her head with the preserver. It wasn't strong enough to do any damage, but it gave me a moment to run to the bow while she figured out what the hell hit her.

When she'd shaken it off and walked toward me again, I was ready. I stood, feet apart, blade in one hand. "Come at me, bitch."

Pausing in front of me, she said, "I've de-fleshed men twice your size, Whitaker. I've ground them up and laid bricks with their bones. You think you're going to do much with that thing? A lifetime, Whitaker. A lifetime of using that same blade in your hand."

"That's sick."

"You call it sick. I call it efficient. Those men were dead anyway. We just repurposed their bodies. It's no different than what we do with animals."

"Except it's murder and nothing to do with animals."

"Tomato, to-mah-to." She shrugged.

"Do me a favor and get rid of yourself, Syndia. The moment investigators see what you've done here, you'll be dead anyway."

"You first, sweetie pie. In fact, that blade works best if you cut your neck here..." She showed me the slanted angle at the base of the neck on the left side. "Blood drains right out. Less work for me. I'd appreciate it."

I stared at her, waiting for her next move. Slowly backing up. Slowly making my way to the spear again.

"You had the chance to leave. Your mommy told you to come home, but you Drudge women, you don't listen. We always have to take matters into our own hands."

"Fuck you."

She was quick when she lunged at me, catching me by the edge of my shirt again and pulling me toward her. Though I gripped at the fiberglass, it was slippery and she was able to heave a blow of her hammer. I ducked out of the way, just as the hammerhead smashed a window in the wheelhouse.

We wrestled, each trying to dislodge the tools from each other's hands, slipping and sliding all the way to the stern again, pushing and pulling, when she swiped her foot under me and knocked me onto my back. Damn it, I couldn't get a break, and worse, she'd swiped the boning knife from my hand and now straddled me, one knee on either side.

"You did it wrong," she said, pressing the point of the blade to my jugular. "It's here. Right here…"

This was it.

I'd done my best, but my best hadn't been good enough.

The spear went rolling against the inside wall of the boat and I imagined my mother at home, worried about me here in the epicenter of Hell. I imagined the little Big Wheel she'd given me when I was a kid, how I played with that thing for months, years. I remembered Nana when she could still walk, still cook and come over to make dinners for me while my mother finished up at her second job.

These women had worked their asses off for me, and all I could do in return was fail.

I'm sorry. I'm sorry…

A bead of sweat dropped from Syndia's forehead into my eye, burning my vision, and at that moment, something swift and instant froze my enemy's body right where she was. Her eyes widened, her body trembled, and thick blood poured from her mouth, dripping off her chin and into my mouth.

I spit the blood back into her face. What the hell?

Behind her, standing on the edge of the boat, holding the end of the fishing spear in her hand, pushing the sharp end through Syndia's neck, was Nottie. Who was not dead. Not in the least. She'd taken a bruising at some point, sure, but otherwise, she was very much alive. Saving my ass…

"I thought…" I couldn't form words. "I thought…"

Syndia rolled off my body and landed on her back like a harpooned starfish, as Nottie yanked the tip of the spear from her neck. I didn't know what in Jesus's name was going on, if I was the next to die, or what. But then, the old woman threw the spear on top of Syndia's chest for good measure and watched as the blood drained from her body.

Here we were, the maiden, the mother, and the crone from my grandmother's drawings in her book of shadows. And the crone had prevailed.

When Nottie sat her shaking body down on the floor of the boat, only then could I draw a breath. "I thought you were dead. I thought you were…" Shock prevented me from forming a coherent thought, but she got the point.

Wiping sweat from her face, she pointed at the cabin underneath the wheelhouse. "I wouldn't help her bring in that man from the pool. She threatened to kill me. She hit me with that hammer, so I run off."

"In the storm?"

"Yes. Been here since this morning."

"In this boat?"

"In this boat."

"But why…why…" I fumbled for words, drawing in my knees. "Why would you help me?"

"Miss Whitaker, for fifty years I worked for this family. Heard the stories. When I began caring for Miss Violet, her senile mind would forget itself and she'd tell me things she wasn't supposed to tell no one."

"What did she tell you?" I asked.

"What *didn't* she tell me." Nottie scoffed. "The more details I heard, the more I knew I was in danger just for knowing them, but I couldn't go. I needed the money." The rain started coming down in sheets just then, washing Syndia's blood like she was one of her fish down by the shed. The bite of salt in the air was strong but felt good. It felt like the storm was over.

"Did you know about their family business?"

"The front or the real one?"

"The real one," I replied.

"I never participated but I knew. They thought it was a secret with all their locked doors but I knew. I cleaned this damned place. Every damn day. The evidence was everywhere. I knew they was operating a house of cards. Only a matter of time before it came down. Your grandma cursed this land."

"So I heard."

"I heard it, too. I was there."

"I'm sorry, what?" I leaned my ear to her.

"With my own ears. I was there. It set off years of misfortune," Nottie said, looking off into the inlet. "But I'll always be grateful to her."

She was there and heard the words? Who was she? "You heard my grandmother?" I asked. "Why? How?"

"Because." She wiped the sweat from her forehead and ran her hand across her skirt. "I was eight years old the day Leanne Drudge left Key West. She couldn't fit her bicycle in the truck, so she gave it to me. It was blue. Nobody ever given me anything before." She looked dreamily at the overcast sky. "I never forgot that."

TWENTY-FIVE

Nottie Francis Parker never wanted to be a nurse.

She'd dreamed of moving to New York City and becoming a ballet dancer. She'd dreamed of singing like Ella Fitzgerald to presidents and dignitaries all over the world and of living in a mansion with great gas lanterns out front and palm trees as tall as a three-story buildings.

But life was tough in Key West for her parents, and she was often alone. While they worked, she played with sticks in the street and chased after her older brother who wanted nothing to do with her and everything to do with the girls from the next street over. She often stood in front of Leanne Drudge's house and stared at it, because it was pink like the inside of a conch shell. Because a baby lived there.

Because the house was pretty.

The thing about being a lonely child, however, was that you saw it all.

She'd witnessed how Mrs. McCardle had talked to Mrs. Drudge, saw the police officer the day he'd knocked on her door to give her the bad news, heard the crying coming from the open window, and smelled the burnt garlic and shrimp.

Sometimes, she'd see my grandmother dancing around in nothing but her birthday suit through those windows, late at night, while playing "catch me if you can" with Mr. Drudge. But it was a playful game between them, and he always kissed her at the end. That always made her smile, since her parents never played that way.

Nottie told me all this while sitting out by the dock a week after the storm hit. Six days after police and investigators tore this property apart after I'd showed them what the banyan tree had revealed. I never said I'd found the gold, because that would've been untrue. They'd told me, because it was legally on Syndia Duarte's property, it belonged to the family. But when they'd contacted Duarte's siblings without giving any details, other than to let them know their sister had died during the storm, nobody wanted anything to do with her.

They knew, Nottie told me.

The siblings knew the horrors and did right to stay far away.

They never wanted part of the curse or the family "business."

The historians came out of the woodwork, however. They all wanted to know. They wanted to meet the granddaughter of the famous boat captain who'd died offshore in 1951, who everyone was almost certain had been pirated by the Havana Ferryboat Captain who'd claimed to find gold that night, though nobody could prove anything. They knew, as Nana had known, that such a captain would never have had a boating accident.

Eight months after my back had healed, after the surgery to repair the tear in my lung, after a few court hearings, the gold rightfully became mine.

I knocked on the door to Nottie's new apartment to tell her I'd share it with her fifty-fifty. After all, she'd saved my life, but she wouldn't accept it. "I'll take enough to live comfortable, Miss Ellie. I'm seventy-five. A simple woman. Don't need to live in a mansion anymore."

And so she'd accepted twenty thousand.

Out of ten million.

A simple woman indeed.

That same day on the bench, she'd told me it'd been Luis's body lying on the dining table. The one I'd seen when trying to spy through the cat door inside the secret passageway. Syndia had gone out in the storm to get Luis and bring him inside before he got buried in debris and disaster relief workers found him. She'd planned on getting rid of his body before the storm was over, same as with my body, but I'd been too stubborn to die.

The inn was declared a total loss. Once the McCardle family signed away rights to it, it also went to the state, and there I was able to buy it on auction. But I couldn't live in it the way it was. Hell no. That place had been hell on earth for so many, but since the day Syndia was killed, there'd been a certain peace on the property.

I'd lingered a while, opening myself up to energy, activity, and spirits.

None to be found.

Though I'd replaced my Zoloft but still hadn't started taking it, the only dreams I'd had had been of my grandparents sharing a kiss out on the dock. Mayai had given me a knowing smile once or twice, but that was it.

No darkness, no evil, no curse.

This house, as from a famous movie line involving poltergeists, *is clean.*

I wasn't afraid to live there. But first I had it razed and rebuilt it over the next year and a half while living in a rented apartment off Duval. Every day I drove over to the new house to watch it be built. I made sure they incorporated my grandfather's mosaic mural right in the dining room as a featured piece, and mason workers were even able to rebuild the broken moon sculpture.

That would go in my garden. My herb garden I'd cultivated using Nana's instructions in her book of shadows. I wasn't sure what to do with them once they'd grown, but I'd learn. I'd made friends with a woman down at a new age shop in town, and she'd told me what all the medicinal properties of the herbs were, how to dry them, make mojo bags, infuse them with intention, even cook with them to bring out the best in my life.

Before this, I had no idea this lifestyle even existed. By some standards, I was considered an eclectic witch by the shop owner's spiritual friends, but mostly, I still felt like myself. Only a new and improved Ellie. A more powerful Ellie.

An Ellie now connected to her true self.

So connected, in fact, that I couldn't get enough information about the island's difficult past and sometimes filled in as ghost tour guide when Sunset Spooks Ghost Tours needed a substitute. I loved taking tourists around spooky Key West at night, telling them all about the weird former residents, the Calusa, the piles of bones, the shipwrecks, and the female ghosts who waited for their seafaring husbands to come home.

No longer the healthy skeptic, I knew Luis would've been proud of me.

The ghosts didn't bother me anymore. They were simply a part of the landscape, their voices in tune with my daily rhythm. I found, if I asked them politely to stay away when I wasn't in the mood to deal with them, that they would.

Key West had become my new home. With its tourists, its history, its roosters running rampant everywhere, its chocolate-covered coconut patties, its key lime pie, its weird but rich, laidback culture, I knew I could live here my whole life. So when the house was finally finished, I didn't rent it out like I'd originally planned, I invited my mother to come down and live with me.

She politely refused, said she couldn't live in a house that'd been built over so much tragedy. She didn't quite get it when I explained that that tragedy had been necessary to release the curse, that now only peace, love, and light lived there.

But it was okay.

She would come to visit soon, she told me.

On the last day of construction, I turned on my gas lanterns, made homemade lemonade and sat out on the front porch on my brand new rocking chair, watching the sun go down in the distance.

Nottie had come to christen the home with me. We clinked glasses and she closed her eyes. "This good lemonade, Miss Ellie."

"I learned from the best." I smiled. Setting the glass of lemonade down on a certain little mosaic table between our two chairs, I stood and picked up the sign I'd commissioned downtown earlier this week. "Want to help me hang it?"

"Sure, I would."

Together, we held up the wooden sign while I hammered a single nail in a column, then carefully hung the wooden plaque over it. I stepped back to look at it. In the evening light with the lantern light casting a warm glow over the wood, the sign was perfect:

CASA DE LOS CAYOS
Est. 1923

The year my great-grandmother had purchased the original home.

199

Taking a few photos of it with my phone, I smiled, satisfied with the way it looked. Then, stepping back up the porch steps and sinking into the rocking chair, I picked my lemonade back up, sipping as we watched the cars roll by. Bacon purred up against my legs. I reached down to scratch his head. "I got nothin', buddy. Nothin'."

Life was perfect, idyllic, the way it'd been in Nana's tales.

In a way, I guess I'd always lived on this tropical island under the sun, even before my feet had ever touched down on it. My childhood dreams had shown me my future and what could be. My soul had always lived at *Casa de los Cayos*—first as Mayai, then as Nana, now as Ellie Whitaker.

It'd just been waiting to come home.

Acknowledgements

I'd like to thank Ted Messimer (Southernmost Ted) of the Key West Ghost and Mysteries Tour for answering research questions. If you happen to be in Key West, make sure to take his informational and fun ghost tours—they're awesome!

I'd also like to thank Jonathan Maberry for a wonderful and inspirational quote for the ISLAND OF BONES book cover. Jonathan, you ROCK!

My critique group— Stephanie Hairston, Danielle Joseph, Christina Diaz Gonzalez, Alex Flinn, and Curtis Sponsler—for providing insightful feedback, especially on that pesky first chapter.

To my Street Team readers, a hearty thanks for reviewing!

And finally, an extra special shout-out to my one and only, Curtis Sponsler (again), for the totally awesome book cover, for the meals made when I couldn't stop typing, for the kids driven when I couldn't stop editing, and for the hand-fed chocolate when I couldn't sleep until this damn thing was finished. I love you, Bebe.

Book 2 – Haunted Florida

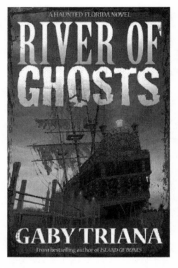

A ghostly pirate ship. A haunted cabin rotting in the swamp. Gladesmen from the Everglades' checkered past.

Avila Cypress gives airboat tours of the Everglades with a little something extra--tales of the supernatural. When a ghost adventures production crew offers her money in exchange for her guiding them to the abandoned Villegas House, a haunted depot with a murderous past in the middle of nowhere, Avila must decide if the opportunities are worth upsetting her traditional Miccosukee Indian family.

As soon as they arrive, strange things begin to happen--disembodied voices, visions of victims long gone, negative emotions. The deeper they delve into the cabin's past, the more they stir up the evil energies. Guests begin turning on each other, and Avila wonders if she made a mistake in coming. Can she develop her untapped gifts in time to save the crew from self-destruction? Or will she become another spirit to wander the River of Grass forever?

Book 3 – Haunted Florida

"Some homes want to be miserable."

A ghostly woman in white. A haunted Victorian home. Witchcraft and Santería from Miami's darker side.

When a mysterious old gentleman enters Kaylin Suarez's trendy new age shop, she hopes he's there to buy incense, some sage, maybe a nice rose quartz pendulum for his wife. Instead, the man pleads for help getting rid of "La Dama de Blanco," a ghostly woman in bloody white dress who has recently begun haunting his 100-year-old Coconut Grove estate.

A newbie witch, Kaylin decides to handle the spirit herself instead of deferring to her paranormal community. When her rituals and spells uncover terrifying secrets hidden in the walls of the estate, Kaylin realizes La Dama de Blanco is only the beginning of the haunted home's evil legacy.

About the Author

GABY TRIANA is the bestselling author of *Island of Bones, Cakespell, Wake the Hollow, Summer of Yesterday*, and many more, as well as 40+ ghostwritten novels for best-selling authors. Gaby has published with HarperCollins, Simon & Schuster, and Entangled, won an IRA Teen Choice Award, ALA Best Paperback Award, and Hispanic Magazine's Good Reads of 2008. She writes about ghosts, haunted places, and abandoned locations. When not obsessing over Halloween, Christmas, or the paranormal, she's taking her family to Disney World, the Grand Canyon, LA, New York, or Key West. Gaby dreams of living in the forests of New England one day but for the meantime resides in sunny Miami with her boys, Michael, Noah, and Murphy, her husband Curtis, their dog, Chloe, and four cats—Daisy, Mickey Meows, Paris, and the reformed thug/shooting survivor, Bowie.

Visit Gaby at **www.GabyTriana.com** and subscribe to her **newsletter**. Also, check out her blog at: **www.WitchHaunt.com.**

Also by Gaby Triana

Horror:

ISLAND OF BONES
RIVER OF GHOSTS
CITY OF SPELLS

Paranormal Young Adult:
WAKE THE HOLLOW

Contemporary Young Adult:
CAKESPELL
SUMMER OF YESTERDAY
RIDING THE UNIVERSE
THE TEMPTRESS FOUR
CUBANITA
BACKSTAGE PASS

Made in the USA
Middletown, DE
02 July 2021

43526136R00125